Totally Bound Publishing books by Genella DeGrey:

Love Divine
Masterpiece
A Touch of Destiny
Sins of the Flesh
Whisked Away
Cat and Mouse
Oasis of Eden
Unmasked
Joust of Hearts

JOUST OF HEARTS

GENELLA DEGREY

Joust of Hearts
ISBN # 978-1-78430-849-0
©Copyright Genella DeGrey 2015
Cover Art by Posh Gosh ©Copyright October 2015
Interior text design by Claire Siemaszkiewicz
Totally Bound Publishing

Published in 2015 by Totally Bound Publishing, Newland House, The Point, Weaver Road, Lincoln, LN6 3QN, United Kingdom.

Totally Bound Publishing is a subsidiary of Totally Entwined Group Limited.

JOUST OF HEARTS

Dedication

Joust of Hearts is a throwback to the classic romance novels of the 1980s. In fact, the first draft of Joust was completed way back in 1995, handwritten on a spiral notepad. The single love scene it originally contained was quite subpar owing to my personal experiences. Funny how life shapes us with both fire and ice as we continue upon the journey.

Though normally I write strong heroines, there were times in history when a woman wasn't able to prevail against politics and greedy land wars without a strong, able-bodied man to protect her.

Here's to the days of damsels in distress and the heroes of old who weren't afraid to risk all to save them.

I would like to give credit to William C. Hurt for the instruction on armor and jousting in this particular time period.

Prologue

Midsummer's Eve, 1500

He is dead.

The three words echoed loudly in Melisande's ears as she poured the required handful of dirt over her late husband's sword and chain-mailed chest. Unchecked, her hand shook violently.

The last few days had been melded together as if forged in a smithy. The time seemed to be without beginning or end. Even the temporary respite of sleep had eluded her without mercy.

Numb, she gazed at the men while they slid the marble slab into place that would serve to seal her husband within his tomb for all time. She clenched her teeth at the discordant, abrasive sound of stone against stone.

Sir Liam Dupree had been a great knight. He had won the day for king and country many a time in his youth, and now he would rest. May God have mercy on his soul.

Will God have mercy on his soul? The thought sent a cold shiver over Melisande's shoulders and down her back. As a knight, he had killed hundreds of men in the service of King Richard, then for King Henry VII. He would at least spend some time in Purgatory, according to the teachings of the Roman Catholic Church. She attempted to pull her cloak closer to her chilled body but found that she was being escorted up the steps and out of the family vault.

Once outside, those whose lives depended upon Melisande and Dupree Castle turned to her for guidance, their sad eyes both questioning and thoughtful. Her gaze scanned each and every face.

So this was what it had come to — the running of the sizeable old castle would now be set upon her slight, twenty-year-old shoulders. She didn't feel twenty. *Nay, much, much older, ancient even.* Her life spent, but not at her own liberty, her youth whittled to naught by someone else's hand.

One of her lady's maids placed a gentle hand on her back and Melisande was drawn from her dim reflections.

The corners of her mouth scarcely lifted in what was her best attempt at a smile on this dark day. "Go to," she said just above a whisper to the population of Dupree Castle, nodding. "We shall endure."

Chapter One

Early Autumn, 1501

The page had intoned loudly as he'd stood in the great hall of Dupree Castle —

To the Lady Melisande Dupree
Concerning the games at Willowbrook.
Please attend and bestow upon us your talents
of voice and instrument
at our day and evening festivities to be held
11 October,
in the year of our Lord fifteen hundred and one.
The Lord and Lady Bergavny.

"Our lady is indeed vexed this day."

Melisande disregarded her maid's impertinent comment as she sat on the opposite side of the solar by the west window plying needle and thread. Maggie and Tilly were two of the most loquacious chits, likely in the whole of England, but she'd learned to pay their discourse little heed. Well, most of the time. They'd been assigned to her upon her marriage and had been her only source as to the goings-on inside the walls of Dupree Castle. Maggie with her wide blue gaze, always the first to bring gossip to her confidante, Tilly. Tilly, with her catlike curiosity and almond-shaped brown eyes, would soak up every word and later confirm the information. Whatever pastime kept them interested in life and no matter what inspired their activities, they were infallibly loyal to Melisande.

"Think you she will change her mind and not want to go to the Willowbrook games?" Maggie beseeched Tilly in hushed tones.

"Nay. Not whilst I have a breath in my body. We have not been farther than the village in an age, and I can no longer abide the stale geldings in Dupree's stables."

Maggie elbowed Tilly in the ribs with a grin.

"Your words, however softly dispensed, do not go unheard past my ears, you know," Melisande admonished her maids, albeit gently.

"Aye, m'lady," they murmured in unison, dipping their matching white barbette-covered heads in submission. They continued to talk amongst themselves, but their volume had lowered considerably for the time being.

Since the first of the previous month, Melisande felt as if she had made a pact with the piper and it was time to pay. She had responded with word of her plans to attend—an act she now found sorely regrettable. Though it had been over a year, she still did not feel ready to face the friends and fellow knights who had fought alongside her late husband.

Nevertheless, because she had responded positively, she should attend. *'Twould be discourteous if I changed my mind and refused at such a late date.*

"One of the miller's sons let it slip that Hamish asked you to take a walk with him tonight," Maggie commented to Tilly. "Didn't you used to see him regularly?"

"Aye, but I haven't yet decided to give him my favor."

"Whyever not?"

Tilly shrugged a shoulder. "He's the one who broke with me last spring. Now that he's made his way round the village he's back, sniffing up my skirts."

"What a lout. And so many like him hereabouts, too. He's a robust lout, but a lout to be sure."

"We will see what the evening brings. I've a mind to change my decision plenty — nine times between now and then."

Ah, to be fickle and free, Melisande mused as she half-listened to their freshly audible banter. However, her station wouldn't permit such frivolities.

Indeed, she was a bundle of contradictions, she admitted to herself. It seemed that none of the people of Dupree had set out beyond the walls of her late husband's stronghold since he had passed away, save the game hunters and those who tilled the earth and tended the crops.

She'd oft wondered how she could ever venture forth without a destination to entice her. Where would she go, to visit her parents? *Never.*

"Have I revealed that it has come to me of late, the tale of William, the blacksmith's son?"

"Maggie, you are some kind of friend who would keep such tasty bits from me! What have you heard?"

Melisande shifted upon her embroidery stool and stabbed her needle into the little handkerchief she was working on. Even to this day, it infuriated her when she thought about her parents and what they'd done. Without blinking an eye, they had bartered away their only daughter of ten and six years to the elderly Sir

Liam Dupree. She had not even blanched when she found out that Sir Liam's age went well beyond her own father's. After all, she had been prepared all her life to marry into land and wealth—for that, she was told, was the making of a good match.

"You are familiar with William—and he is handsome to be sure. But when a diligent farmer's daughter sought his company, and beautiful I hear she was, he shunned her."

"Nay!"

"Aye. He promptly took up with some strumpet, who, from what has been told to me, wasn't at all pleasing to look upon, but would agree to a toss in the hay as quick as you please."

"I've heard of this poxy wench, before. S'wounds, my ears hear but my heart, it seems, wishes to deny!"

"Indeed." Maggie nodded. "The man must have no control over his cock whatsoever to be planting seeds in such odious territory, when instead he could have had such a prize."

As Maggie and Tilly chatted between themselves, she paused in pulling her thread through her embroidery hoop when she recalled how eager her parents had seemed to be rid of her. Pinching the needle between her fingers, she pushed it through the fabric once again and a soft growl emitted from her throat.

She caught Maggie's and Tilly's concerned expressions via a single glance their way, but Melisande refused to feel shame for displaying her emotions so.

"So, after the light skirt ran off with someone else who'd struck her fickle fancy, William set off to find the farmer's daughter and try to rekindle her ardor."

"And?"

"All for naught, I'm afraid. 'Twas too late. He'd already broken the farmer's daughter's heart and she would have none of him, nor his apology."

"Serves him right that he shouldn't get the beautiful, well-to-do, smart girl, but have to settle for a lonely bed. I abhor men who think they can sample every girl in the shire, only to decide later on which to take to wife."

"Leaves every last one of us dismayed."

Melisande shook her head. *What's done is done – to all of us, I suppose. And we have naught to say about it.* The fact of the matter was that Sir Liam had paid for her hand instead of requiring a dowry. Sold, to the lecherous, violent Sir Liam—by her own parents. That had served to sour her taste for *ever* seeing her relations again. Shaking off the familiar feelings of pain and guilt, she continued with her task.

"I can no longer abide the cold, wet kisses of Harold, now that I heard tell that he coupled with that same harlot whom William took up with," Maggie complained.

Tilly agreed. "Aye, and the trouble with Frederick is that he wants to give his kisses to every girl he comes across, just like the rest of them. He said as much, too, the rogue."

"'Twould be heaven itself to find the one man who wanted only me."

Clearing her throat, Melisande attempted to quiet her maids, so she could think.

One of Melisande's original excuses for not attending the Bergavnys' festivities was that she hadn't a thing to wear. The loquacious pair, who were each less than two years younger than Melisande, had persuaded her to take the journey by working day and night on four beautiful new robes for their lady. She had known, however, that the encouragement was not without ulterior motives. It was as if every season was spring and her maids were rabbits.

Melisande sighed aloud.

"Is aught amiss, m'lady?" Tilly tipped her head, her brow wrinkled with concern.

"Nay. All is as it should be," Melisande placated the girl. She knew her servants meant well, but at this moment, she'd like to be left to herself to struggle with her fears and wrestle with the ghosts of her past.

Attempting to bring her attention back to needle and thread, Melisande's thoughts again wandered back to her late husband.

Although Liam had insisted that theirs was a love match, to Melisande it had been in actuality duty. Duty to her family, though they were thoroughly undeserving.

"…with *child*. Just think on it. No help from the culprit forthcoming!"

Tilly shook her head. "And she never heard from him again?"

"Nay, the arrant, black-souled knave."

Again Melisande stabbed at her cloth, but this time she pricked her finger. A ruby drop formed and she quickly stuck the abused digit between her lips to remove the blood before it stained the fabric. Bloodshed from the toils of garment embellishment was, quite truthfully, the only variety she could abide.

Despite the hurt Melisande felt from having found out her parents had practically taken her to market like a cow from the barn, she had decided to be the best wife she could for the venerable Sir Liam. That should at least account for *something* in the Kingdom of Heaven.

"I know naught what the boys are about these days."

"Does one give in or does one keep the secrets of her heart from them?"

"The dangers fall on both sides. Danger of loving and losing, or danger of never loving at all."

"I wouldn't mind loving so much if I didn't lose my heart in the process."

Melisande's four short years of marriage had been spent listening to Sir Liam and his talk of the glory days from his past. He'd spoken of the battles fought, the dismembered bodies that lay rotting on the battlefields, the weapons, the strengths and weaknesses of every armorer in Christendom and their methods of forming and forging—it was his life's blood, the way in which he had made his fortune. *Praise be to God the nightmares of death and violent battles abated not six months ago.*

By the time Sir Liam had realized that life had more to offer, a wife, children at his feet, family traditions to be made, it was nearly too late for the elderly knight.

She was brought out of her musings by a statement from one of the girls.

"...and she never did find her underskirt. Who knows where it ended up?"

"That girl couples with anything with a cock."

The girls tittered together like a pair of nanny goats.

Disregarding the unladylike comment, Melisande sank back into her thoughts. Her wifely duties had been the most embarrassing part of the marriage. Nay, not discomforting for her, but for him. Although Liam had been very vocal about his attraction to her, Melisande had had to do quite a lot of coaxing for his member to join her in the once or twice a month marital rituals. His culmination had come...some of the time.

Melisande was secretly glad that she had not produced an heir for him, although the thought riddled her with guilt more oft than not. She knew that Liam had been a harsh and immovable man despite his age, and would have taught their sons how to fight and kill. Of course, honor would have been imparted, which would have been all well and good, but if it had come with the rest, Melisande would not have wanted any of it.

"M'lady, what say you to this?" Maggie enquired, holding up the beaded collar.

Melisande glanced up and immediately back down to her rosebud border. "Aye, Maggie, 'twill serve."

"M'lady, we are still going on the journey, are we not?" Tilly asked timidly.

"I..." She paused, not sure how to respond, as she'd been back and forth with herself with the subject all day. "I've not yet come to a final decision."

Maggie and Tilly exchanged looks.

Once again, Melisande overlooked their harmless insolence as she continued upon her mental path. In the year after her husband had passed on, she had vowed never to marry a fighting man like Liam again. She had wealth, and from what Liam had told her, her family was secure. Melisande supposed it was time to start living life. However, her prime stumbling block was that she did not know *how* to start living life — what to do, where to go from here. It was much simpler, not to mention more practical, to stay home and oversee the running of Dupree Castle.

The probability was high that at the Willowbrook games some of the Bergavnys' guests would bring to conversation things she'd hoped to forget — such as the great age difference between her and Liam — and ask her how she was feeling now.

"I am nearly finished. Naught but the trim left."

"I have that much as well, and soon we shall have our answer."

Melisande paused in wonder at the extraordinary events of her past. After the funeral, she'd felt that the situation in which she'd found herself was yet another lesson from God, instructing her to depend upon Him. However, her faith was solid, she had spent many hours in prayer asking for direction. Then, right away, the daily routine at Dupree had taken over and her fears had diminished regarding her soul's destination. As the months went by, she'd felt as though she had been delivered both spiritually and physically from marriage to Liam. She was head of her household and had the respect of everyone around her.

Regardless of her feelings, in every circumstance, when speaking with the servants or in the privacy of her chambers, Melisande did her very best to respect the memory of the great Sir Liam Dupree.

Here at home, Melisande had been alone with no one but the servants for company for what seemed like an entire lifetime. She felt comfortable with the way her life had turned out. With her attendance at the Willowbrook games, she would have to face the Bergavnys and, likely, her past.

With her kerchief now complete, she set it aside and joined Tilly and Maggie in the beading of a surcoat.

"Remember when Lord and Lady Bergavny came to visit?" Tilly enquired of Maggie.

"Aye. They broke in every bed in which they slept," Maggie scoffed.

"That will be enough," Melisande warned.

When Liam was alive, Melisande thought it probable that Lord and Lady Bergavny had tolerated her only out of consideration for their friend. However, on occasion, the couple would ask her to recite poetry or play a musical instrument for them while they visited Dupree.

Always the brightest part of her married life, Melisande had loved to perform for their guests as well as for Liam. Since she was a child, Melisande had relished the gift of memorization and very much enjoyed sharing her abilities before an audience, large or small. Her musical skills were unmatched, according to Liam. Why, she could pick up practically any instrument and play it proficiently. Then there was her speaking voice. That alone would have been a sufficient enough ability, for she could boom like thunder or tinkle like little bells. It was intense yet elegant, resonant yet feminine, and carried well to everyone in attendance. Liam had made certain to vocalize his opinion on the matter. She recalled how he'd always been sweetest to her after a presentation.

Tilly made a sudden shift that brought Melisande back to ponder the situation at hand. Not only was the Bergavnys' summons an initial request to present her talents beyond the walls of Dupree, but it was also the first social invitation she had received since her husband's death.

* * * *

That evening, when the last of the seed pearls were sewn into the fourth surcoat, Melisande made the announcement that they would in fact be attending the games at Willowbrook. She instructed the girls to pack the trunks with her new wardrobe and a few of her instruments, and have everything loaded onto two wagons for the journey.

After assisting Melisande into her nightshift, Maggie and Tilly walked serenely out of the chamber. Once they had shut her door, she heard them running down the hall, giggling like children. But what did she expect? They were in great need of fresh company and news from beyond Dupree's walls.

Melisande lay awake in her bed, hoping she would feel differently about the Bergavnys' event as time passed. This tossing about served to disturb her peaceful existence and stir up all kinds of memories she wished could have remained buried. Perhaps she would become excited about seeing people other than the inhabitants of Dupree Castle. Melisande sighed, doubting very much that anything would change her heart about the games at Willowbrook.

* * * *

Quietly, so as not to awaken the randy woman, for she would surely arouse him yet again for another tumble, Devin drew the hem of his doublet down over his hose-covered thighs and slipped from the room.

She'd been adventurous, to say the least, but had he stayed until the dawn, it might have been his undoing.

He'd ridden hard the day before on his way back to Willowbrook and had made it nearly all the way. But he'd found himself drawn in by the come-hither smile of a noble woman who just happened to be stopping at an inn situated near a public drinking well at the last major crossroad before home.

Then he'd ridden her hard for most of the night.

In reflection of the situation, he grinned. His tastes had become much more refined of late. The higher up in social status he reached for his pleasures, the more creative he'd had to be to entice the women to join him in bed. Not that it was difficult, but a wealthy woman required more than a rakish smile and show of strength. Well, most of them, anyway. Of course, not the one from last night.

He hadn't enquired, but he was certain she was a few years older than he. It was no secret that a mature woman's body was capable of unparalleled heights in bed, and she was no exception. In addition her generosity, coupled with her eagerness for him, had set him at ease and made coupling with her quite pleasurable. She'd offered to pay not only for the best room the innkeeper had, but for his meals and two casks each of wine and beer, too — far more than even he could consume. And he'd been known to outstrip bigger men than himself in drinking games, even, on occasion, one after another.

If his confession was sought by a priest, he'd be obliged to admit to the man of God, after the admission of his sins, of course, that with every passing year, a night spent in revelry took longer to recover from the next day.

Devin shut the door quietly, grinned and shook his head. If he could find an unmarried woman who delighted both his mind and body, he'd surely have a prize.

He ordered his horse saddled at the inn's stable then headed north. By nightfall, he'd be home. His squire, Devin was sure, would be keeping watch for his approach, for the start of the Willowbrook games was but a day away.

Chapter Two

Melisande, Maggie and Tilly climbed into the wagon her late husband had had completed just days before he'd passed on. This would be its maiden voyage, for Melisande had never fancied the thought of venturing forth beyond Dupree's walls until the invitation to the Bergavnys' had been issued.

The small procession left for Willowbrook just as dawn was breaking over the horizon.

The journey was slow, for the paths were rarely visited. The shrubbery on either side practically choked out the course and the caravan seemed to gouge its way through the old passage. The ruts, stones and deep mud puddles from the last rains were harsh on the horses as well as the large wooden wheels of the three transports. More than once Melisande had hope that something would greatly affect their trip and the party would have to turn back... But to no avail.

They finally arrived at the Willowbrook gates at dusk that very day. As Melisande's drivers unloaded her trunks, she was shown along with her maids to their chambers in the old castle.

The Willowbrook servants brought to her chamber a lavender-scented basin of water for her in which she could refresh herself. After Melisande had partaken of the meal delivered to her room at her behest, Lady Bergavny herself made an appearance. The woman was taller than Melisande, yet still petite enough to be called fragile. 'Twas her age that made her so, for she was mayhaps forty and five. Though her head and shoulders were covered by the cream-colored barbette she wore, it was still transparent enough to reveal the many strands of silver hair mixed in with the black.

"I am truly pleased you have decided to attend the games, Melisande," Lady Bergavny said warmly. "How have you been faring, my dear?"

Melisande smiled as she took the lady's proffered hands. "We are very well at Dupree. Gramercy, Lady Bergavny."

"And your journey?"

"The route was greatly in need of a drying by the sun. However, we arrived in good time."

"Splendid. Fitzherbert and I are most anxious to hear what verses you will be presenting at the opening of the games on the morrow."

"I have chosen to recite *Sir Gawain and the Green Knight*. Bravery and adoration for a damsel are intertwined beautifully in the tale."

"Oh, Melisande, 'twill be a most perfect selection, for the men as well as the ladies will enjoy the telling."

"I do hope for that to be the tribute you receive," Melisande replied with sincerity.

"Of that I am certain."

"May God grant you mercy, Lady Bergavny," Melisande said as she disengaged her hands and executed a curtsy.

"Melisande, there is no need be so formal, and do call me Helena," she announced with a bright smile.

That statement alone made Melisande feel slightly better about being out in public for the first time in so many months. She found it quite comforting to have a friend and to feel safe so far away from Dupree. "I shall then, Helena."

"Delightful. Anything you are in need of, enquire of my servants."

"Thank you again, Lady—Helena."

Helena nodded in acknowledgment. "Sleep well. I will have my attendants alert your maids as to when to awaken you." She reached out once again, giving a reassuring squeeze to Melisande's hands. Just before stepping out of the room, she said, "I pray that you enjoy your holiday with us. I look forward to the morrow." And she pulled the heavy oak door closed.

Maggie helped Melisande into her sleeping gown while Tilly arranged the bed coverings. She then climbed the two wooden steps and lay in the middle of the down-filled mattress. Sleep, she knew, would come soon, so she bade the maids snuff out the candles.

Finding herself once again anticipatory about Liam's allies, whom she was to meet over the next two days, Melisande silently meditated as she closed her eyes. *In two days hence, I may return home. I count the hours.*

Tired from the tedious journey, and mentally exhausted from worrying overmuch, she slept hard through the night.

* * * *

As her maids rushed into the room the next morning, Melisande felt slightly disoriented at first glance of her surroundings.

"We were unable to awaken thee for the mass, m'lady, and the games will begin shortly. 'Tis past time for you to rise and meet the day," Tilly said in haste.

Ah. Now she remembered where she was. *Willowbrook.* The thought ran through her mind that she should just pull the coverlet back over her head and stay there for the rest of the day. At Dupree, Melisande had arranged for mass to be said each day after ten of the clock, owing to the fact that she usually slept best past the rising of the sun.

Maggie placed a slaver of bread and cheese onto the bed. "Do eat, m'lady, and we shall dress you directly."

After the last crust of bread was down, and Melisande was sure it wouldn't come back up owing to her misgivings, the maids chose a light green and ivory outfit for their mistress. Melisande, not in a disposition for pastels, disallowed the decision and made them dress her in a dark gray tunic and matching surcoat. Decorative ribbons of the same hue fell like streamers from the soft white leather belt just above her waist.

Maggie and Tilly worked collectively to tuck Melisande's hair into a silver-gray chaperon. As they finished, a knock sounded at the door. Melisande stood, smoothing out the ribbons along her waist. She called permission to enter.

The large oaken door swung open and there stood an elderly male servant dressed in Willowbrook colors. "The lord and lady have requested Lady Dupree to join them on the Bergavny pavilions, directly. It is my duty to escort you."

"Very well." Taking a deep breath, she started for the door with Maggie and Tilly in tow.

As they made their way along the battlement wall, Melisande gazed out over the expanse of the property. There were hundreds of people assembled to witness the events, not counting the large number of servants running behind and around the tents, decorating them with the family crests and blazons of their lords. Liam had tried to describe to her how many attendees would be present at the games, but it was altogether different seeing it. Melisande was sure this was the greatest number of people she had ever seen at a singular gathering in her entire life. *All from the nearby villages must be in attendance this day.*

From afar, she witnessed the beautifully decorated banners and flags caught high in the wind to the east and west of the lists. Willowbrook Castle was to the north of the festivities, a good walking distance from the commotion.

Melisande and her maids followed as their escort passed lovingly tended gardens and intricately carved stone benches placed to garner the best views. Then they traversed over a small meadow of tall grass with a wide gravel-strewn path curving through it. They finally came to the lists and the Bergavny pavilion where the Lord and Lady of Willowbrook were seated. Draped in Willowbrook colors, the structure was built high above ground on a platform big enough to hold three large chairs and a small handful of servants.

Before Melisande ascended the final six steps to the main deck, she dismissed Maggie and Tilly. "You may have the rest of the day to yourselves. However, I shall require you in my chambers this e'en." The two maids curtsied and scampered off.

When Melisande reached the dais, Helena spoke. "Come, sit here with me." Helena patted the large, ornately carved wooden chair next to her and turned to her husband. "Fitzherbert, you remember Lady Melisande Dupree?"

Melisande curtsied to him.

"Indeed, indeed. How it warms my heart to see you, Lady Dupree." He smiled.

"You look well, Lord Bergavny," Melisande replied with a respectful nod.

"I thank you, my dear. As do you."

After she was seated, Helena whispered, "My lord is very pleased that you have come to Willowbrook."

Melisande glanced at her host. Lord Bergavny was of good health, at least better than Sir Liam had been in the few years Melisande had known him. Lord Bergavny had gray hair that reached to his chin, and, at present, came from underneath the folded rim of his black fur hat, blending with his matching beard. He had kind blue eyes that peered out through slits from under bushy white brows. His fine robe was a richly embroidered soft green fabric with a wide brown fur lapel that complemented the lighter brown of his hose. A large gold medallion and thick chain were draped around his shoulders. A great ring of gold bearing the Bergavny seal perched regally on his right index finger.

Melisande's gaze shifted to the center attraction. So this was the lists she had heard so much about from Liam. She was loath to see any bloodshed, or horses' eyes rolling with fear, or anything that would bring forth the bad dreams of which she was finally rid. She remembered well the tales of her late husband and his victories on the battlefield. *I pray Thee, Lord, deliver me swiftly through this day.*

Helena placed her hand over Melisande's. "You look pale, my dear." She then added, "I have not seen you unnerved as you are now, just before you recite. All will love the chronicle you will share — you may be assured of that." She patted Melisande's hand gently.

Melisande made an effort to smile at Lady Helena, for it was in fact not her performance she was concerned with. It was being here at the blood-games, which seemed to cause so many people amusement, and having to witness them first-hand.

Almost everything that surrounded Melisande reminded her of Sir Liam. *He thrived on this kind of living,* she thought with a shudder, the sandy lists, the large crowds that emitted strange odors when many un-bathed people and animals came together, the anticipation of the games. Luckily for her, Sir Liam had been too old to travel around the country from tourney to tourney by the time they were married. Sometimes, though, she felt as if she *had* lived this way because of the many, many stories she'd listened to at her husband's feet. Occasionally she'd wished she had not the lucid imagination that accompanied her memorization skills.

Trumpets gained the attention of the audience and everyone quickly found their seat. The herald introduced Lady Melisande Dupree as a bard of yesteryear. Melisande stood up. After the crowd's shouts and huzzahs subsided, she began the verses of *Sir Gawain.*

Chapter Three

Devin's fellow knights, in the midst of being readied by their squires, departed from the tent in haste. Before he could ask what they were about, he noticed the sudden silence of the crowd assembled for the joust. Curious, he followed. Such cognitive matters claimed his wits more oft than naught. He supposed it to be a flaw in his soul.

As they approached the lists, a single feminine voice talking of knights and ladies floated toward them on the wind. Two of the men elbowed one another and estimated that the voice must have been attached to a beautiful face in order to gain the vast assemblage's attention thus.

Satisfied, the two made their way back to their dressing tents, all the while teasing the others about the fair maiden and who could win her.

Devin moved to a place where he could get a closer look at the young lady. It was times such as this that he was glad to be a head taller than most of the men. A slight breeze blew a few strands of hair across his eyes.

He smoothed the hair away from his face and swept his hand over his whiskers, scratching as he went.

He focused in on the visage that belonged to the melodious voice and held his breath in order to still the mesh-against-metal noise his chain mail made when it rubbed against his tassets. It was certainly not because he found her to be most comely, although the rapidly growing bulge against the protective padding behind his codpiece begged to differ.

Her voice, though loud enough to be heard by everyone, was like a caress to him. She seemed to look right through him as well as her entire audience. Her eyes were a silvery-gray, an exact likeness of the color of her attire. His gaze refused to falter from where it had landed, and all surrounding her lovely face faded to black, as if she were at the opposite end of a long tunnel. He felt suddenly warm as he stood motionless, watching, listening.

God's teeth, you're not some green lad, he chided himself. He'd flirted with and bedded many a fine-looking maiden, why did his body react to the storyteller thus? He found himself randy as a spring morning. One side of his mouth curled up in a grin. He could have her if he wanted. This one was a mere performer, she must be used to such amusements... But he'd have to find out for sure before he began his pursuit. He thought to ask his squire to find out if this goddess would be at the banquet this eve.

The applause and shouts of the crowd woke him from his thoughts. The young lady's face flushed with a reddish glow and she curtsied in appreciation of their approval and attentiveness.

It was her blush that made his heart skip a beat. It was genuine, not feigned or painted on like those of the women at court.

He had only been to court once, which was quite enough for him, he had admitted on several occasions. The smiles and eyelash fluttering of those women were as stale as yesterday's loaf. He'd ridden half of them anyway, and what good was it? The married ones had willingly spread their legs for him, but it was as if they had all received the same instruction on bedding. There was no creativity in their chambers. He would just as soon apply needle to thread as go back to those boring women.

He redirected his focus to his next conquest. *Fie, but she looks as soft as a feather mattress covered in silk.* If angels looked as if they were female, *this* girl just might be one.

"Sir Devin! Sir Devin, I must make thee readied! The joust is first! Did you not hear me when I called out?"

Devin dragged his attention from the Bergavnys' pavilion. Parker had made it clear time and again that he was more than thrilled to have been Sir Devin Blackburn's squire for over three years now. He was ten and four—almost five, he had warned many a man who dared to comment on his age of late—and he wished to be a duplicate of his lord. Parker was getting taller by the day and had a fair amount of muscle already developing on his young body, owing to all the jobs Devin would find for him to do around Willowbrook. His brown hair was left just long enough to reach his jaw line, and most of the time was kept tucked behind his ears.

"Aye. Excited are you, Parker?" Devin enquired, knowing full well that Parker lived for the games.

"For certain, it has been too long. Come, we must return so I may get thee armed."

At the armory tent, Parker adjusted the chain-mail tunic so that it sat properly laid over the padded doublet, then tied Devin's vambraces onto each arm.

Devin stepped away, took a few strides forward then returned to Parker's side.

"Is the fit well?"

"As I said before, if I can walk, you've employed my metal skillfully." Devin ruffled his squire's hair.

Parker batted his hands away with a muttered curse.

After Devin's horse was saddled and suited, Parker helped with Devin's helmet, but not before Devin took one final glance toward the Bergavnys' dais.

Likely referring to the storyteller that held Devin's attention, Parker warned, "She was pleasing to look upon my lord, but mind thee about the games. A knight needs not a maid to distract him."

Devin chuckled. "You, Parker, have much to learn yet. There is none so satisfying a distraction as a beautiful woman and the promise of evening pleasures that sparkle in her eyes."

"Has the great Sir Devin, the Black Knight, been reading poetry, then?" Parker mocked.

"I have no need of poetry when the truth will suffice. Now gather my lances or next time I come across a leather-bound manuscript, I shall throw it at your head."

His squire laughed and vowed to continue their verbal repartee on a more convenient occasion.

The participating knights on horseback assembled in front of the pavilion as if Lord and Lady Bergavny were the King and Queen. All knights gave a salute with their swords. Then the lord leaned forward and raised his hand in approval.

Fitzherbert turned to Helena and asked, "Whom shall you favor this day, my love?"

"'Tis a difficult task to choose but one. Perhaps Lady Melisande would take my place in the championing of a knight?" She turned to Melisande with a gleam in her eye.

Melisande's stomach lurched in shock. "In sooth I could not," she refused politely, not wishing to be disrespectful to her hosts.

"But I insist. Come, come. Whom shall you choose?" Helena persisted.

Fitzherbert spoke to Melisande beyond Helena in a mock whisper. "My dear, 'tis always wise to follow as Helena instructs, that is what I find," he said, mirth ringing in his voice. As Fitzherbert reclined back in his chair, Helena stole a sideways glance at her husband and kissed the air in his direction. The love they shared, even at their age, was unmistakable.

"Very well then, I shall do it for *you*, Lord Bergavny." Melisande nodded a bow.

From her belt Melisande pulled a dark gray satin ribbon. She stood, looked over the knights and pictured her shriveled-up husband, barely able to sit erect enough to see out of the sights in his visor. All were polished and adorned with colorful plumes on their helms, and emblems on their mighty shields. One of the knights wore blackened chain mail. In fact, his entire suit was such, save the silver etchings and roped edges. His plume was black, his coat of arms was mostly black—though the outline of the snarling panther's head was white—even his dark gray stallion was draped in flowing black satin. Between the rider and his horse, they seemed to match her pessimistic mood perfectly.

Melisande stepped forward and crooked her finger at the knight in black. He moved his mount next to the platform and leaned toward her. She bent to meet him halfway and tied the ribbon at the base of the black plume of the knight's helm. The knight backed his steed away from the pavilion and saluted the lady whose colors he now wore.

The salute was magnificent. The knight grunted a command to his steed and the horse tucked one of his front hooves under while stretching his other front leg as far forward as was possible. When the horse's nose practically rested on the ground, the knight remained upright in the saddle, holding the hilt of his sword over his heart. All those along the lists were stunned into silence. When a few moments had passed, the knight grunted a second command and the horse returned to its upright position. After an explosion of cheers from the crowd at the sight of the tribute to the Bergavnys' guest, the other knights paraded around to gain favors for themselves.

"Splendid choice, Lady Dupree, and how fortuitous. The Black Knight is Willowbrook's finest warrior," Lord Bergavny commented.

"Oh." Melisande placed her hand at the base of her throat. "Would you have preferred that I'd championed one of your guest's knights?"

"Nay, my dear. You may choose whomsoever you wish," Helena said in a comforting tone.

Helena's support did not make Melisande feel any better. Was she condoning the violence by championing the knight? Melisande sat back in her chair and covered her face with her hands.

"Something ails you," Helena insisted and placed her hand on Melisande's knee.

Melisande raised her head. "It must be all the excitement of the day," she assured, not letting on to the truth.

"If at any moment you must excuse yourself, Fitzherbert and I shan't be offended."

"I thank you, Helena, all will be well now." The last thing she wanted was to worry them.

Lord Bergavny motioned to the trumpeter to summon the first opponents. The herald announced the men by their colors and the entitlements they held.

A knight with green and yellow plumes sat atop his ornately decorated mount at the north end of the sand-covered field. The Black Knight and his steed were positioned and ready at the south.

"See how each studies their rival in order to find a weakness to use to their advantage?" Lord Bergavny enquired, the excitement in his voice evident.

Melisande squirmed in her seat, preparing for the worst.

When the herald lowered his upraised arm to begin the charge, they started forward, gaining speed as they approached the center.

To Melisande, the sound of the wooden lances splintering against the metal shields was deafening, and she quickly placed her hands over her ears, muffling the sounds of the thunderous crowd as well. The knights received new lances from their squires and made ready for another pass. As they met in the center at full speed, the Black Knight angled his shield so that his challenger's lance skidded off the smooth surface. The Black Knight swiftly grabbed the averted lance and, with a sharp tug, proceeded to unseat his opponent. It had happened so fast that the crowd's reaction was delayed. A moment later, a great roar of approval went up from all around the lists, drowning out Melisande's cry of anguish for the unseated knight. Streamers, banners and handkerchiefs were waved in the air in a celebratory frenzy.

The Black Knight turned to salute Lord Bergavny. To Melisande he placed his gauntleted hand over his breast in salute. She almost missed the gesture, for she was overly concerned about the yellow and green plumed knight being helped up by his squire. She raised her hand in recognition just in time. If either Lord or Lady Bergavny had been paying close attention to Melisande, they would have indeed noticed her disquiet, for she was sure it showed on her face. She relaxed just enough to settle the bunched muscles from her head to her shoulders, but was unsure as to how long she could keep up the charade.

The rest of the jousting matches went mostly the same way — the Black Knight unseating all of his rivals in one way or another by the second or third passes, and gaining more *atteints* toward victory.

Everyone seemed to be having a most wonderful time — except Melisande, who now felt like her shoulders were part of her ears. At one point she had been gripping the arms of her chair so hard that her hands ached. When the dinner hour came, food was offered to Melisande, but she refused it.

"Melisande, what is the cause of your vexation?" Lady Helena asked. Both she *and* her husband were looking to Melisande now, their concern palpable.

She tried to put her feelings into words, but it was too difficult. Lord Bergavny had his personal valet fetch a flagon of wine for her.

"Are you not having a pleasant day?" Lady Helena enquired, more privately this time.

Melisande was about to express her feelings when the valet appeared and placed the wine into her hands.

"Drink. You will feel the color in your cheeks again in no time," Lord Bergavny assured her.

It was announced that the sword fighting competition was to be next. Melisande gulped down half of her wine at the declaration.

Over and over again, Melisande tried not to look at the fighting, but could not help herself. She was loath to see any blood, but could not tear her gaze away. The sound of steel against steel held her rapt attention.

From directly across the lists, Devin watched the terrified maiden. *What is it that makes her thus frightened?* There was nothing for it but to find out for himself.

The match going on in the lists between the knight in blue and the knight with the brass cross on his breastplate was so intense that no one had noticed Devin step up to the platform. He saw that Lord and Lady Bergavny had the best view of the games, so he stood and watched for a time.

A sudden light breeze caused a feminine fragrance to blow across his face. He drew the scent in on a deep inhalation and his gaze wandered from the lists to the Bergavnys' guest. She must have been a lady, for her robes, upon such intimate inspection, appeared to be expensive. She also had the hands of a lady — soft looking, with clean, long, elegant fingers. Oh, aye, she was most certainly a lady and not just a hired entertainer. With a grin he couldn't help, he wondered if her hands were as talented as her voice.

Finally, the blue knight bested his opponent and a cheer resounded all around.

Devin left the Bergavny pavilion and made his way back to Parker.

"Thou art next, Sire! Where had you gone? I looked to the privy and — "

"Parker, calm yourself, 'tis not a battle we fight."

"Pray forgive me, m'lord, in sooth, 'tis the excitement of the games! It fairly gives me gooseflesh!"

"Aye, it shows so plainly on thy face," Devin teased. His squire Parker was a late bud about to bloom, and at any moment would discover the young maidens who hid behind corners watching him. Devin figured that Parker's passion for life would surely sweep him away when that day came. Perhaps he should hurry it along and give Parker more time to himself. This in turn would give Devin the opportunity to get to know Lady Helena's guest.

While Parker proceeded to ready him for the next match, Devin thought about what was making the young lady so upset. The only sights that he had observed from behind her were the sport upon the lists. That had to be it. *She is not amused by the fighting*. It suddenly became perfectly clear to him that it was the games that made her greatly ill at ease. There was much to consider if Devin were to be presented to her. He would have to make sure that no one mentioned to her that he had participated in the games today. That profession would have to come later, if at all.

Chapter Four

Melisande downed the last bit of wine as the Black Knight and the burgundy-caped knight took their places and bowed to their lord. Lady Helena gained Melisande's attention and suggested they go have an early supper together while the games were finishing.

"That is most considerate of you, Helena. If you would rather see to the finishing of the contest, I could go alone."

"Nonsense. I have confidence that one of the Willowbrook knights will triumph and be dubbed best in all of Christendom by Fitzherbert." Helena smiled and took a quick peek at her beloved, who caught the action and winked at her.

"You seem to know these procedures well." Melisande felt relief flood through her veins like a simmering brew.

"Indeed I do. Now, I for one am famished. Fitzherbert plundered the last half of my game hen, leaving me naught but the bony carcass."

For several seconds, Melisande merely gazed at Helena. By and by she realized Helena was but jesting.

She allowed a bubble of a giggle to escape from between her lips, the first since she'd left Dupree Castle.

"Let us see what we can find to eat, lest I faint from hunger," Helena added, then took Melisande by the hand, leading her toward the food pavilions.

* * * *

Melisande ate her fill and saw that Helena had done the same. She sat back in her chair and stretched her hands above her head, a very unladylike motion, of course, but she didn't give it a second thought. "I think I could fall asleep, so full is my belly."

"Mm," Helena agreed. "I, too, could use an early evening rest. To be honest, I could miss the hunt without any remorse whatsoever."

Leaving the table and tent, Helena walked arm in arm with Melisande up the path to the keep, then escorted her to her guest chambers. "Do not sleep too late, my dear. Give your maids enough time to ready you for the feast and rounds this eve."

"Oh. I did not realize dancing was planned for this evening's entertainment. I am sure I do not have the proper gown for the event." Melisande drew her hands down the front of her skirts. She'd be most grateful to be excused, thereby bypassing the occasion altogether.

"If this were the only gown you had, I would say to wear it, for it is most lovely. But, alas, I was informed of your three trunks of clothing..."

Melisande folded her hands before her and lowered her gaze. She wasn't going to get out of the dancing as easily as she'd hoped.

"Pray forgive me, Melisande, I was too harsh. Most insensitive of me." She stepped forward in an affable manner and lifted Melisande's chin with her fingertips so that their eyes met. "Melisande," she said, speaking softly, "your mourning has passed, you have allowed enough time to grieve over Liam. He was Fitzherbert's friend, too. We both understand the loss. However, you are very young yet. You need to experience more of what life has to offer. Tonight you will meet some very honorable men that I am sure Fitzherbert and I would approve of. You need to socialize with your peers and I will be there for you if needs be. Now, smile and promise me that you will attend."

She had to admit, she'd indeed been lonely for attentions from members of the opposite sex, a thought she had pushed to the back of her mind many times over the last year. Much to her dismay, Melisande's eyes began to water as her forlorn sentiment overwhelmed her. Was it that she felt guilty for not being overly sorry that Liam was gone? Was she truly afraid of meeting other men? Was it the emotions of the day that kept her so tense that she was now exhausted? Or was it all that put together? "You practically know my every thought, Helena," she said as two errant tears spilled down her cheeks.

Helena hugged Melisande. "Your fears will pass, I vow. Rest now, before the eve is upon us."

Melisande pulled out of Helena's arms, nodded, then wiped her tears away with the backs of her hands.

"We shall see you in the great hall for the feast, and no more crying. We do not want to attend with our eyes puffy," Helena said from the portal of Melisande's chamber with a kind smile.

"Aye, Helena." She reached out and closed her door.

* * * *

Melisande awoke from her brief repose just after the sun dipped beyond the realm and the last of the day's colors clung in the clouds over the horizon.

Maggie and Tilly were not in the antechamber, nor were they in the immediate vicinity. Opening her door, Melisande called out to a passing serf to fetch her tardy maids.

Shrugging off her feelings of frustration, Melisande headed for her trunks. She chose her lavender robes with the beaded bodice and velvet underskirt in dark blue. The sleeves of the robe were lined in sky-blue silk and were as wide as they were long. The collar of the robe dipped to a subtle 'V' and was covered in seed pearls. The small headdress she chose was also in blue, with cream-colored gossamer veils that fell just beyond the shoulders. The matching cream sleeves of her chemise reached to her wrists and fit her arms snugly. These robes were her favorite, for both her maids declared that they made her eyes more blue than gray.

Maggie and Tilly came rushing into the room, pouring forth their apologies. They quickly dressed Melisande, and praised her for her beauty and taste. Melisande ascertained that they were only trying to avoid reprimand for being late.

Her ablution complete, Melisande made her way down the winding stone staircase that led to the great hall where tables were set for supper. The large room was lit with hundreds of candles and housed nearly as many jovial guests.

Helena had a seat waiting for Melisande at the high table. "Come, Melisande. The hunt, it seems, was a great success and there is plenty on which to sup."

As she sat, a trencher and flagon of wine were placed in front of her. She smiled, made small talk and endured introduction after introduction to lords and ladies, young maidens seeking husbands and an occasional elderly knight or two.

Devin could hardly eat. He blocked out all table noises and other voices except *hers*. Her laughter was as magical as her smile.

"Aye, Lady Dupree, recount once again some verses for us." A voice sounded from one of the other guests at the high table.

"Aye!"

"We would be most appreciative!"

"Pray do, my lady."

Pleadings abounded all around.

Helena spoke up. "The evening's verses were going to be said after we have danced a while, but if you wish it now —"

"Prithee, my lady!"

"Oh indeed!"

"The amusement would gladden us greatly!"

Devin found himself caught up in the enthusiasm. "'Twould be most welcome," he agreed. The man next to him chimed in as well.

Melisande stood up and cleared her throat with a swallow of her wine. "I have chosen some verses from *Cursor Mundi*, which was, as you may know, written during the year of our Lord thirteen hundred and twenty."

As she spoke, it was as if she transported her audience back in time. Her voice fluctuations and pronunciations of the old dialect were perfect. When she finished, the whole room lit up with robust applause and shouts of "Huzzah!" Fists and goblets were struck upon tabletops.

Lord Bergavny's smile practically illuminated the room. "This evening's festivities are going even better than I could have hoped for." He beamed, and instructed his pages to clear away the tables. Helena bade another servant call the musicians to the gallery for the dancing.

When sufficient room was made in the great hall, Lord Bergavny turned to his wife and held out his hand. "Shall we make our way to the floor, my dove?"

"Aye, my lord," Helena replied. She placed her fingertips upon his knuckles, briefly skimming his skin in an unspoken amorous gesture. Devin had never envied anyone as he did Lord Bergavny at that moment.

As the musicians readied their instruments, the guests assembled in the center of the room and paired off for a circular dance.

Devin started toward Lady Dupree to ask her to dance, but some rutting stag of a boy snatched her up instantly. Devin narrowed his eyes at him. However, the boy missed the reprimand, so enamored was he with the Bergavneys' guest. Had he been a fellow knight, Devin would have challenged him right then and there.

His anger took him aback, but only for an instant. In order for him to participate, he needed a partner to equalize the count of men and women. He proceeded to ask the closest maiden to join him. She accepted with enthusiasm and he hoped belatedly that the girl's mother did not presume that this was the beginning of her daughter's future. She placed her hand on his and they moved toward the other dancers.

In all honesty, it was Lady Dupree he wanted — and so much so that he ached with it. The last time a woman affected him so was his first sexual encounter. It had taken him an entire two weeks to talk her into a tryst. The next morning, when her father found them in the barn, naked and in each other's arms, the man sent her to a nunnery. Devin had been drunk with her beauty that night, and so young... He'd known what he'd done was a sin and guilt had riddled him for an entire month or more.

However, this interest in the storyteller wasn't gluttony or drunkenness, merely the vice of lust, which, now that he was an adult and in total control of his actions, usually didn't last beyond one or perhaps two nights between his object's thighs.

His cock surged at the very thought of sinking into Lady Dupree's creamy heat.

The lines were formed with men on one side, the ladies on the other, each directly across from their chosen partner.

Melisande admired the beauty of the gowns that danced before her. The vivid colors and sparkling jewels were resplendent even in the dimness of candlelight. The gentle rustle of silks that could be heard around her would be an inspiration to gown designers at home and abroad. She coyly glanced down the line of gentlemen in their finery and wondered how Lady Helena knew so many handsome men.

The dancers went forth, changing partners as the music dictated. Melisande glanced up and her breath caught in her throat. Her newest dance partner was one of the most handsome men in the room. He looked at her with such a pleasant intensity that she heated under his scrutiny. He was tall with light brown hair and eyes the color of a meadow at the peak of spring. His hands were large in comparison to hers, strong yet gentle, which echoed the rest of his build. His face was smooth and youthful, save for the few furrows between his brows, denoting deep concentration. No man had ever looked at her the way he did... It appeared to be a challenge and an invitation in a single look. They broke apart and continued down the line to their next partners.

Melisande was both startled and delighted. She swept her gaze down the line of men and became drawn to her previous partner's pleasing form and graceful steps. She could not wait until she passed him again. *What is this*? she thought to herself as she tried to conceal her smile. *A joust of hearts, with only your wit and eyes as weapons?* As he approached, Melisande failed in her attempt to stop her body from shaking in anticipation of when their hands would touch once more. Thanks be to God that it didn't take long to come round to him again.

He took her hand and pulled her closer than was customary for dancing. "You look thirsty," he said, his voice silky smooth. "When the music ends, would you permit me to fetch you some wine?"

"I'm afraid we have not as yet been introduced. Had I known you from Adam, there would not exist an impediment," Melisande said loftily. She would not allow this man to know that she was already curiously attracted to him.

"I am Devin, you are Lady Dupree. Needs there be more said?" he stated with much authority and confidence.

Devin. She sighed inwardly, maintaining an outward appearance of indifference for propriety's sake. "You, sir, are forward in the extreme." She raised her chin in defiance and cocked an eyebrow for emphasis.

He leaned closer yet to her ear. "And you, m'lady, do not seem to mind overmuch," he replied with a wicked grin.

Feeling as though he were reading her mind, Melisande detected heat flooding her entire body. She couldn't help but grin in surrender. *Do my thoughts show so plainly on my face?* She surmised that she was sorely out of practice when it came to conversing flirtatiously with men. 'Twas the security of her friend's home that afforded her the luxury of agreeing to his suggestion, she supposed. Sighing audibly, with a nod, she answered, "Very well, I shall permit you."

Devin's smile shone his victory. "Meet me in the garden, my Lady Dupree," he whispered as they broke apart again.

Chapter Five

Melisande's thoughts whirled and her heart pounded in her ears. She realized she had changed partners twice more before the music ended and hadn't said a word to either one of them. Before the next melody began and she was caught up in another round, Melisande headed for the doors that led to the gardens outside. She'd nearly reached them when she passed by the Bergavnys.

Helena reached out and placed a hand on Melisande's shoulder. "Are you enjoying yourself?"

"I am finding this eve more to my liking with each passing moment," she whispered in a rush to Helena and patted her hand.

Helena lifted an eyebrow and a mischievous smile parted her lips. "Excellent, Melisande. Most excellent."

She excused herself and continued toward the garden doors. A confidence settled upon her she usually only experienced when holding an audience on the edge of their seats during a crescendo or a most intense moment of a chronicle. After all, they were going to be in public. *What could happen that would be considered wrong?* On the other hand, what if something did happen? A grin tugged at the corners of her mouth. *So what if it does? This Devin is a most handsome man, and it has been so long...*

Melisande passed through the door and started out toward the moonlit gardens. Devin had his foot propped up on a stone bench, a goblet of wine in each hand. As she approached, he came to a more formal standing position.

She could see the silhouette of his shoulders by the silvery light of the moon and at once he seemed much bigger than she remembered. Slightly less than two arm's lengths away, she felt her aplomb slip and turned back to the entrance of the hall.

"Lady Dupree, please don't leave."

Melisande halted and shut her eyes.

"I have brought the wine needed to quench your thirst." His voice held an odd sort of supplication and yet rang with promise.

She decided she was thirsty and, after all, he'd only asked her to share a drink with him. Melisande cringed inwardly at the thought of being such a prodigious tangle of contradictions, but then again, hadn't that always been her predicament? She opened her eyes and slowly turned toward him, noticing an unlit torch close to the bench behind him.

"Why has the fire been doused? 'Tis difficult to see," she commented, meanwhile, in the back of her mind, she searched in earnest for a suitable conversation to begin with him.

"Pray forgive me. The couple that occupied this bench, before I dismissed them, had already put the flame out. I had not a free hand to start it burning anew. Shall I—"

"Nay, verily, there will be no need. I-I feel safe as long as you are here with me." Merciful heavens, it sounded to Melisande as if she were listening from without, rather than participating in the discussion.

"Do you?" Devin's smile revealed his straight, white teeth regardless of the near-darkness.

"Why, of course..." Melisande said, nervously walking forward and taking the goblet from him, accidentally brushing her hand over his. Devin's smile faltered slightly, but she was sure it couldn't have been from the contact of their skin. "You simply asked me to join you for refreshment." She heard her own voice speak as if she were trying to convince herself. With a slight shake of her head, Melisande put that idea as far from her thoughts as she could and gracefully lowered herself to the bench. A brief, nagging opinion flitted through her mind that she really should not be here with a strange man, however handsome. She stole a quick glance his way.

Handsome, she found, was an understatement.

Devin sat beside her and she watched him take a quick sip of his drink. "Unless there is something more you desire," he said, setting his wine down on the ground next to the bench.

Melisande took a large gulp of her wine then started to stand. "Nay, what else could there be?"

Devin reached out and caught her by the waist. He gently pulled her down onto his lap, her back against his chest. His breath warmed her neck and stirred her hair. A thrill buzzed through her like a bee flying in haste to his hive. She listened intently as Devin inhaled deep into his being.

"Let us explore those possibilities," he whispered as he took her goblet and set it down next to his own.

"I—" Melisande began to protest, but at the same time, she felt heat creep up her back and gooseflesh crawl down her arms. At once, a boldness swept over her that she had never dreamed existed. Her discontent now cast aside, she leaned her head back to rest on his shoulder.

For a brief moment, Devin tightened his hold on her waist, his way of conveying a silent approval, she imagined. Then he glided his hands up either side of her ribcage and slid forward until his fingertips grazed her breasts.

At the first bolt of pleasure, Melisande lifted her head abruptly—part of her startled, part of her blissfully astonished. She refused to think as she maneuvered her legs around so that her feet were now resting next to him on the bench.

He slid one of his arms underneath Melisande's knees and his other hand pressed into the small of her back, pulling her closer still. A groan reverberated from the man in whose embrace she was now captive.

She smoothed her hands up his fabric-clad, muscled arms and to the back of his neck, where her fingers tangled in his hair.

She looked into his eyes. The torchlights coming from the doors of Willowbrook's great hall flickered in them. It made the moment seem like an illumination from some magical realm.

Devin leaned his head toward hers and gently took possession of what he sought.

Melisande's eyes had closed, seemingly of their own volition, when his lips touched hers and a thousand flaming arrows sparked from behind her lids. She felt his hand float from where it sat at the small of her back along the silk of her dress and around to her side and beyond to 'explore the possibilities' of her breasts.

Liam had touched her many, many times before, but it had *never* felt like this.

Devin removed his other hand from under her knees and deftly slipped it beneath the neckline of her gown. His fingertips came in contact with her nipple. As he plied his fingers to the sensitive flesh, her moan reverberated against his mouth.

Melisande pulled away from the kiss and pressed her cheek against his, her breathing sharp and rapid. Suddenly the world shrank to include only herself and this beautifully bewitching man. She didn't want to think, only feel. Her senses reeled out of control and yet were so focused. First she grazed her lips across his cheek. *So smooth.* Then she touched it with the tip of her tongue. *Salty-sweet.* Inhaling his scent, she became aware of his hand as it pressed hard against her beating heart. What would it be like to have his entire body unclothed and melded against her own, flesh to flesh? She placed little kisses across his cheek until she found his ear. She left a tiny kiss on his earlobe then drew the flesh between her teeth, teasing it with her tongue.

He stilled his hand and she hoped it was because of the sensation she was causing as she explored him.

"You are heating the very blood coursing through my veins to molten steel," he whispered.

"Melisande. Melisande?" A voice called out to her from far away, pulling them from their cocoon of intimacy. He hissed an inhalation through his teeth and she groaned, both unwilling to be thrust back into reality.

"I want more."

She could detect a sort of passionate pain in his words.

"And I want more time with you as well." Melisande couldn't bring herself to openly confess to him that she felt as if she'd discovered a new world—a world she very much wanted to further investigate.

"Melisande?" The appeal was much louder than before.

"'Tis Helena and she's coming closer." His hand slipped from inside her bodice as she leaped from his lap.

"Wait—" He attempted a protest but she wouldn't allow herself to be caught in such a base position by Helena.

"I am here. What do you require of me?" Melisande called out, her voice higher in pitch than normal.

"Come, join the other musicians and play your lute," Helena said from somewhere in the courtyard.

She mustn't find me here like this! Panic threatened to overtake her. "I will be there directly," she promised, straightening her garments.

Devin stood. "Must you go now?"

"Aye, I must. 'Twas the lady herself who called for me. Are you coming?"

"I have not had that chance yet."

"You—" Melisande clamped her lips shut, catching his jest a little late. She peered up at him as she hurried by and caught his grin in the dim light.

"Fear naught, Lady Dupree. I shall join thee by and by."

Inside, Melisande still felt short of breath as she approached the other musicians. One of her maids had brought down her lute and set it on a stool for her upon the gallery. She wanted to get this over with, for she felt that everyone saw the color of fire in her cheeks that likely accompanied the heat radiating from her person.

She half-heartedly played through the piece. At one point, she looked up and saw Devin leaning against the portal to where they had been unchaperoned. Her hands shook through the rest of the arietta.

The audience applauded. Melisande curtsied and made her way quickly to Helena.

"That was splendid," Helena complimented as she took Melisande's hands and pulled her closer. Lowering her voice, she said, "I can tell I have interrupted something. Do forgive me. I shall be more cautious in the future."

"I know naught of what you speak," Melisande denied, sweeping aside unseen wrinkles from the front of her robes. *Did I think I could hide my behavior from this woman or anyone else for that matter?* Guilt threatened to overcome her. *Dear God, I should never have…*

"So, I see you have met our special guest," Helena said over Melisande's head.

Melisande whirled around and came face to chest with Devin. Her eyes made a gradual ascent to meet his. She tried to swallow, but her dry mouth would not permit it, so she gave him a polite smile.

Devin returned her smile with triple the enthusiasm. He handed her a goblet of wine, the one he'd taken from her so they could embrace. She took a sip as she couldn't think of anything to say.

"Aye, we exchanged…words."

"Then you know Devin is —"

"Very anxious to get back to our conversation." He finished Helena's sentence and looked down into Melisande's eyes pointedly.

Lord Bergavny joined the group and asked Melisande for the next dance just as she opened her mouth to respond to Devin's brazen comment.

Melisande swallowed her discourse, which she knew would surely have put Devin back in his place. "I would enjoy that very much, Lord Bergavny," she replied, passing the goblet back to Devin and tearing her gaze from his. She felt a barrage of emotions assault her. Devin had gotten away with far more verbal insinuation than was polite. *He is awfully arrogant. How could he have hinted like that to Lady Helena, of all people, that we were having a 'conversation'? Why, it simply reeks of tomfoolery.* Melisande refused to have Helena think ill of her. She pushed all that aside for now and managed to smile at Lord Bergavny.

"Pray excuse us." He nodded to Devin and Helena, and Melisande placed her hand atop his proffered arm.

Devin watched Melisande being led toward the other dancers. Thinking quickly, he passed the used goblets into the hands of a passing servant, and turned to Helena. "Would you permit me, Lady Bergavny?" He lifted a solicitous elbow to Helena, which she took.

"I shall, Sir Devin." She smiled then added, "You have shaved your beard. I don't believe I have seen your chin since first your whiskers grew in. How long has it been? Mayhaps a score of years or so?" she cajoled with a sly grin.

Devin chuckled and looked out toward the others preparing to dance. "Surely not a full score, my lady, for I am not yet twenty and nine."

Helena laughed. "You know I do but jest. I remember when you came to us as if it were yesterday. It was just days after Henry VII was crowned King of England, and you were a young squire having aided Fitzherbert and his allies in the battle for Willowbrook. I recall when Henry gave the castle and its immense property to Fitzherbert. However, there seemed to be a bit of confusion over ownership."

"This is one of your favorite stories, my lady, or have you perhaps forgotten that I was there?" Now it was his turn to taunt her.

"Aye, indeed, you impudent boy." She grinned then sobered. "It was also the most frightening time of my life. But once the day was won, Fitzherbert requested of your sponsor that you stay on at Willowbrook with us. He agreed and, as young as you were, Fitzherbert knighted you in tribute of the victory."

"It was and still is an honor I shall be eternally grateful for." He bowed to her, but as the music began, his thoughts strayed. After much training and once he became of age, he'd traveled from Willowbrook to some of the more local tourneys, then to London, applying his skills of riding and wenching, as was his wont to do.

The king had initially wished to reward his comrade just after Bosworth, and had offered a dukedom to Fitzherbert. He had been honored by the king's generosity. However, he'd explained to Henry that it was his fervent wish to retire without being tied to the tasks that accompanied the offered rank. Henry had sympathized but, regardless, given Fitzherbert a peer's title.

Several steps into the dance, Devin glanced around to find Melisande.

As the ladies followed each other in a close circle, the men circumnavigated in the opposite direction from without.

One of the ladies addressed Melisande. "Will you be joining us for dinner out on the east lawns at noontime tomorrow?"

Melisande looked to Helena, who followed behind. Helena nodded.

"I will be in attendance, aye," Melisande confirmed, and inclined her head at the woman who had enquired.

"Will you be entertaining us further?" one of the other women asked.

Melisande again looked to Helena for an answer to the question and Helena spoke up. "Melisande is a guest here at Willowbrook as you yourselves are. She will not be performing at every turn."

"Oh aye."

"By all means."

"We do agree."

After a few moments passed, Melisande spoke softly to Helena. "After these rounds are finished, would you escort me to my chamber?"

"Of course, Melisande. You are not feeling ill, are you?"

"Not at all. Merely tired."

The women expanded the circle to intertwine with the men.

As Devin passed Melisande, he whispered, "I must see you tonight." Their gazes never left each other's as they threaded their way through the other dancers. She shook her head, hoping that he understood her refusal.

They met again. "But why?" he pleaded quietly.

"I have had my fill of sinful deeds for one night, thank you very much. Now do not speak of it again," Melisande whispered back in a rush.

When the dance ended and they honored their partners all around, Devin leaned toward Melisande. "Then when?" he asked quietly.

"On the east lawns at the dinner hour tomorrow."

"The dinner hour?" he asked, puzzled. Melisande nodded and he added, "But all will be in attendance."

Melisande looked into his lush green eyes and said aloud, "Precisely," then lowered her head in accompaniment of an elegant curtsy.

Helena came and took Melisande by the arm. As they passed Lord Bergavny, Melisande thanked him for a wonderful evening and, in turn, he thanked her for sharing her talents. The two ladies started up the stairs and Melisande did not wish to yield even the slightest glance toward Devin. She could, however, feel his warm gaze upon her person.

The two women reached the top of the staircase and Helena paused to comment about the look on Melisande's face. "You look...rather... Well, very—"

Helena was obviously at a loss for words, but at the moment, no words was exactly what Melisande wished for. They began the ascent up the narrow stone stairs toward her chambers.

Melisande tried to comfort her hostess. "Truly, I had a wonderful time, I am just tired."

"Fitzherbert and I are concerned about you," Helena said, placing her arm around Melisande's shoulders.

"You need not be, truly. Go, dance the night away and be merry. You and Lord Bergavny seem to be so in love. Do not take that for granted," she said as they reached her door, just before Maggie pulled it open for Melisande.

"You are wise beyond your years, my child." The elder woman smiled.

"Goodnight, Helena." Melisande dipped her head in a polite bow then she stepped through the door.

Tilly and Maggie helped her undress. They chattered between themselves about the different men they had met and which ones they would like to get to know better. Melisande dismissed the young chits and blew out the candles herself. Used to an even cooler chamber at Dupree than Willowbrook's walls afforded, she decided to move aside the large tapestry and open the shutters for some fresh air. Once this was accomplished, she climbed into bed.

Melisande was drifting into a satisfying slumber — in truth, she was even more tired than she had admitted to Helena — when she heard a noise that seemed to come from outside on the allure below.

Through the barest of slits in her parted eyelids, upon the ledge she could see the tall figure of a man leaning against the partition that separated the twin portals in the wall, his shoulders just touching either side of the one he filled. Melisande knew exactly who it was. *Devin*. How dare he come to her room like this, and how long had he been standing there? If he took one step in, she vowed she would scream to high heaven.

Chapter Six

Devin watched Melisande as she slept in the moonlight, gazing upon her halo of hair fanning out across the pillow beneath her head. His insides felt as if they were plummeting to his feet. She seemed so pure, so real. God's teeth, how he longed to climb under that coverlet and just hold her. *Nay*, he admitted with a shake of his head, he wished to do more than that... *Much more.* But she was asleep. He daren't awaken her, for he knew she'd never forgive him for disobeying her wishes about not wanting his company this night. For as much beauty as she possessed, she had a headstrong disposition. *What sort of attack could break down such defenses?* He almost laughed aloud at the idea. He'd never even thought to adhere to the concerns of the other women he'd been with. He'd never had to. They'd wanted him and he'd wanted them. He'd never lingered beyond the coupling, had never had to make pleasant conversation. The arrangement had always been simple.

He focused on Melisande once again. Suddenly *nothing* was simple.

Pretending to be asleep, Melisande did not move at all during his perusal of her, which, to her, seemed to go on forever.

Of a sudden, he stood up straight. Melisande flooded her lungs with air, ready to shout in alarm. However, he reached up and placed the tapestry back over the window as if shutting a door, then he was gone.

Melisande sat up in her bed, and the scream she'd prepared was hastily puffed out of her mouth in silence. She threw the coverlet off and dashed over to peek beyond the tapestry. It seemed that he'd vanished over the wall.

"That was the extent of his visit?" she said aloud, suddenly wondering at the discovery that she'd actually wanted his company so late at night...in her chamber. Her indecisiveness vaulted emotions over the edge from victim to huntress. A very disappointed huntress. More vexed than before, she slammed the shutters closed, bolted them, flung the tapestry shut and marched back to bed, stomping her feet on the hard floor, kicking at rushes all the way. "Honestly, men are the most frustrating creatures," she murmered to the empty room. She pulled her pillow over her head and, in a huff, went to sleep.

* * * *

"You have slept late again, m'lady. If you did not love your sleep so, I am sure Maggie and me would be labeled a disgrace by the others who share our tasks."

"Oh, Tilly, do not fuss so," she mumbled from her stupor and opened her eyes with caution. They'd moved the tapestry so that the sun beamed into the room, illuminating everything to a visual screech. She sank deeper into the warmth and darkness of her bedding.

Maggie pulled the covering from Melisande's face. "Now, you will be needing to break your fast. I shall fetch a salver before all is swept away." She hurried from the room.

"Your light green gown and ivory robes will do fine for the tour and dinner later this day. Which headpiece would you prefer, your green chaperon or the ivory-horned headdress?"

Resigned to the invasion, Melisande sat up in her bed and found that she had a slight headache. "I will not be wearing a headpiece, Tilly. I would like a braid."

"But, m'lady, everyone will be wearing a head covering of some sort," Tilly whined in a tone that made Melisande want to place her hands over her ears.

Here was yet another battle she didn't care to attend. Besides, she was at the home of a friend, not at court, for heaven's sake. She should be able to take her ease if she so desired. "Bring me the one I wear for Mass."

Tilly did as she was told and returned from the trunks with the hat, handing it to her mistress. Melisande proceeded to remove the length of long sheer white fabric from the headpiece. "We shall fasten this to the top of my head for a covering. Will that suffice?"

Perhaps if Maggie had been there, Melisande would have drawn more argument from her maids. Together they, at times, were a formative pair. She supposed they only did it for her sake and for the sake of appearances, but there really was no need. Not at Willowbrook.

After Melisande ate the bread and meat Maggie had brought up, the girls dressed her and began dressing her hair. They wove the braids at the front on both sides of her head to form a crown, then joined loosely at the center to fall down to her waist. With the thin handle of a wooden comb, Maggie meticulously tucked the folded material into the front of the crown. Then she lifted the fabric off Melisande's face and let it hang from the crown to halfway down her back. Tilly and Maggie both agreed that this was more practical and feminine than the other head coverings.

Melisande wondered if Devin would like it then, just as quickly, pushed that thought aside.

* * * *

Lord Bergavny was speaking to a group of twenty or so when Melisande finally joined them. "This day we shall take a tour of Willowbrook and her grounds. I myself will escort you to the stables, to the gardens, and finally through the great hall that is the heart of Willowbrook. I shall share with you the history of the battle in which I fought to obtain this property" — Lord Bergavny paused then continued with much puzzlement — "which seems to not have been so many years ago, unless one would study a chart of years."

The group chuckled.

Melisande was not looking forward to *that* part of the tour. *These knights are all the same,* she thought to herself. *Always talking of their former days of glory.*

At once she became aware of a presence behind her. She spared the intrusion a quick glance. How could she have thought it would be anyone but Devin? Why, she could practically sense his virility. After all, she had felt it when he stood just inside her chamber the night before, even from across her room. Facing forward again, she adjusted her sleeves.

"Good day, Lady Melisande." Devin spoke softly, close to her ear.

She was sure he knew the reaction he caused when he breathed his words so near. A flash of memory presented her with the vision of Devin upon her chamber's ledge, and Melisande seemed to transform into a saucy creature, one over which she had no control. "Good day to you, Devin," she said, turning fully to look up at him. His handsome face nearly made her knees buckle. Would he catch her and pull her into his big strong arms? *Get hold of yourself, Melisande.* She mentally tried to shake off her lustful thoughts and contradictory feelings. Her thoughts would insist upon one thing and out from her mouth came the opposite. *The battle going on inside between my body and mind... Why, no knight, no matter how strong, could stand up to its force.* Of this she was certain.

The group started forward following Lord Bergavny, and Devin continued to speak close to Melisande. "You are a pleasant sight to look upon this day, my lady."

"And I was not last eve?" she asked raising an eyebrow, hoping to draw from him confession and summon as many smart retorts from her own lips as possible.

"I wanted to do more last eve than look," he purred into her ear.

"You *did* do more last eve than look," she whispered sarcastically, even though her heart threatened to pound its way out of her chest. *Oh, how this man excites the senses.*

"Aye, and you were most agreeable." He placed his hands on her waist from behind and gave her a squeeze.

Melisande felt unsettled. The control of the situation seemed completely out of her hands now, and she wiggled away from his grasp. "Mayhaps. Now be still that I may hear what Lord Bergavny has to tell."

Much to her relief, Devin did not speak again until they left the stables. Quietly, from behind, he offered, "Did you dream of me after you retired?"

"I... I never remember having dreams," she lied. In her dream he'd come back through the portal and made love to her. *He'd no doubt enjoy hearing that*, she thought wryly. Melisande folded her arms in front of her to stop her hands from shaking. She was thankful that he could not see her burning cheeks.

"You visited my dreams. Would you like to hear of it?" he enquired, stepping so close that the tips of his boots became lost under the hem of her robes.

She tried to pull away. "I am sure I would not be interested —"

"Oh, but you would." Devin caught her by the arm and made her face him.

"Very well, what type of gown was I wearing?" she asked, yielding to his insistence. At least now he would have a topic to stick to, and not wander back to the indiscretions of the night before.

He slid his palm down her arm, lingering at her wrist. "You did not wear a single strip of cloth in my dream," he admitted, just above a whisper.

As fast as lightning she spun away from him, but Devin leaned his chest forward so that he was gently pressing against her back. She could feel the heat of him through their garments. "Nothing but your golden hair covered my pillow as we lay there together."

In an attempt to escape Devin's insolence and equally brazen topic, she cleared her throat and hastily searched for a subject to present to the lord of the manor, "Pray tell us, Lord Bergavny, have you any plans for additions to your gardens?" Melisande blurted a bit too loudly.

Devin chuckled softly as she strode a pace away from him.

Lord Bergavny went on and on about his ideas about stone pathways, fountains, topiaries and the like.

Melisande desperately wanted to look interested, and at the same time was trying to control her capricious composure. This man Devin simply had to appear and she was taken completely out of her normal character.

She wanted to remove her outer robe, for the heat seemed to rise from the ground. Then Melisande realized that they were standing in the shade. It was Devin that warmed her, mind, body and spirit. He was a danger to her very existence as she knew it.

Melisande folded her arms across her chest and pressed her lips together. She heaved a breath noisily out of her nose. *Why do I lose my self-possession so easily? What have I become – some wanton kitchen wench?* she silently chastised herself. *What of my good Christian morals? Surely I have those to lean upon when trouble arises. I must repent and drive these demons away.* As resolute as she could be at the moment, Melisande offered up to heaven a quick penance accompanied by a plea for strength. She hoped it would be enough.

Lord Bergavny finished the tour of the gardens, and was presently drawing the group toward the castle.

Melisande supposed she shouldn't have remained at the back of the group. *'Twas much easier for Devin to stir up mischief.*

As they walked along the battlement wall, Lord Bergavny began the telling of the taking of Willowbrook. Melisande finally gathered the courage to look up at Devin, who now stood next to her.

He spoke before she could. "See you the large parapet at the top floor of the west-most wing, sweet?"

Melisande shielded her eyes from the sun. "Aye," she replied, inwardly bristling over the endearment.

"That is where I sleep. If you ever have need —"

"And what, pray tell, would I need from you in your chamber?" she enquired none too quietly. Here it was, her first skirmish with Lucifer when it was just moments ago that she had looked toward heaven to help her.

"Shhh... Quietly. You wouldn't want everyone watching when you come to me."

"When I— You have some fanciful ideas." Melisande's head fairly swam with the notion. She promptly pushed her thoughts aside and jerked her chin in the opposite direction. She tried in vain to regain control of her senses. At his next words, her gaze flew back to meet his.

"If you but knew," he said, grinning down at her.

Clearly, her tattered nerves could not take much more of this. She made to protest. "Well, I do not —"

"Indeed you do, my lady," came his smug retort.

"Ha. You have nothing I need." Melisande felt that her feeble reply could not have possibly repressed his verbal advances.

And why did you have to be so handsome? At once, Melisande was certain she had lost the battle, for on her face, she knew, shone the betraying thought as if she had spoken it aloud. And much to her misery, she could see that Devin had already absorbed each fanciful word.

She turned her back to him in a huff. His flirtations were too much for her to bear, not to mention that her experience with enticing, charismatic men was non-existent. This man was far too tempting. She could never win at this game and she was a fool to have thought otherwise.

Devin leaned close to her ear and whispered, "I know you have not had a husband in over a year. You do have a need whether you admit it or nay, and I wish to fill that need."

Merciful heavens. This battle was now all but lost. Melisande's legs went weak, and she leaned back against him and closed her eyes. "You make love to me with your words and confuse me so." She couldn't be sure if she'd actually voiced her thoughts aloud, but what did it matter?

Devin wrapped his arms around her, kissed her neck and whispered back, "I have much more to offer than mere words. Come to me this night."

"I-I mustn't. 'Twould be a sin," she replied quietly, her breathing gone ragged.

He nuzzled her neck as he spoke. "Melisande, we have already succumbed to our need for each other and I, for one, am loath to sustain the punishment without having indulged in the sin."

The low tones of his voice reverberated in her ear and she clutched at the skin on her arms to calm the gooseflesh. Before her flashed a particularly sensual scene from her dream that made her very existence seem to spin out of control.

But what will happen upon the morrow? Melisande knew not if it had to do with her plea to heaven or her own reality raising its voice, but it wrenched her from her private fixation. "I depart at dawn. I would never see you again, and I am not inclined to endure another loss in my life," she said flatly. As she opened her eyes, the crushing fact swept over her like the trampling of a great warhorse. Melisande nudged out of Devin's embrace and walked back to the stairway that led off the battlement wall. Managing to control her senses, she raced down the steps, wishing to be free of her demons.

Chapter Seven

As the distance stretched between him and Melisande, Devin could feel the joy that had radiated from him moments ago shrink away like a fading sunset. A strange pang resonated through his heart. Did she still truly mourn her husband after so much time had passed? He could not bear the thought of this petite girl enduring the pain of this or any other loss for that matter. Something needed to be done. Melisande's happiness would have to be secure if he were any sort of chivalrous man, let alone a knight.

Devin endured the rest of the tour without Melisande. He enjoyed hearing of the battle he had squired for so many years ago. And it was indeed a good thing that Lord Bergavny didn't call upon him for comment. His thoughts of Melisande distracted him at every turn — the clever way she bantered with him… Even when she contradicted herself. She could be saucy and, in the same breath, could border on pious. Whatever her reason for such verbal vacillation, it intrigued him. His desire to take his time and unravel her mysteries nearly overwhelmed him.

At the conclusion of the tour, Devin departed in search of Lady Helena. He wished to ask her to convince Melisande to stay on a few more days at Willowbrook. "A few more days," he chuckled as he spoke the words aloud, crossing the inner ward. He had a mind to follow Melisande wherever she would venture — there were no limits, as long as she was there. This game of his had turned into an extraordinary need to possess this sweet wench. Surprisingly, he didn't mind in the least. He couldn't see himself with any other woman, ever.

Devin paused in wonder at the path on which his mind had wandered. "God in heaven," he murmured to himself as the realization of his feelings surged through his being. 'Twas a surprising revelation... Akin to the knowledge of how to defeat an opponent upon the lists. He just *knew* she was the one.

Devin found Lady Helena in her solar, embroidering. Most of her female guests were in their chambers preparing for the dinner out on the east lawns.

"A word, my lady?" Devin asked from the threshold of the room.

She glanced up from her sewing and her astonishment showed on her face for a brief moment. "Sir Devin, what an honor. Please do sit with me." She indicated the upholstered bench across from her.

He sat, not knowing where to begin.

After a few moments of silence she teased, "Has the word you wished to share eluded you?"

Devin chuckled at her ready wit.

"Perhaps you wish to learn the finer points of needle and thread?"

He shook his head, his gaze settling upon the ground between them.

"Then what troubles you? Is it perhaps...a lady?"

Just how she surmised his plight he knew not. He looked up at her. "But how —"

"Female intuition." She answered his unfinished question with a grin and a wink.

So, you can face a blade or mace without so much as a blink, but in these matters you shrink away like a coward? He chided himself before he drew in a breath and forged ahead. "I am concerned about whether the Lady Dupree is finished with her mourning."

"She is. And just."

He nodded. "Well, I was… As it happens, I… Do you think that perhaps…?"

She placed her sewing in her lap. "You wish to win her heart, Sir Devin?"

Devin blew out the trapped air from his lungs. "Indeed, my lady. Her heart and eventually her hand — *if* she will have me."

Her grin was radiant. "I could foresee this. You would make a fine match." She paused, then, after tapping a finger on her chin a few times, continued far more sober a manner than a moment ago. "Devin, there is something I wish to explain to you. A few years ago, when Melisande was younger, she seemed to have a…fire in her eyes." Helena observed her embroidery for a moment then lifted her gaze to Devin. "'Twas after she was married for a few months that that fire died down to more of a…smoldering."

Devin could only nod, encouraging her to go on.

"I cannot explain the situation any more accurately than that. Her eyes do not have that certain something she possessed in the past. Please do not misinterpret my intentions, I adore the child as if she were my own." Helena sighed. "Mayhaps what I am saying is…that I could not abide to see her hurt. You understand, do you not?"

"I do. Melisande's beauty is the finest I have ever beheld. However, it is everything about her that has hold of my heart. I see the 'smoldering' of which you speak and wish to fan that fire, bringing her to life once more."

He watched as Helena considered him for a moment. "Such pretty words from the much feared Black Knight," she commented, ever the jester.

Devin's face heated and he chuckled. "Feared or not, said pretty words are swift to evade my mind when summoned on purpose."

"It oft-times will happen that way, dear boy," she said with a gentle smile then added, "Very well. I shall try to persuade Melisande to remain for a time." She returned to her sewing. "'Twill be quite a task, though—that young lady has ideas of her own," she warned.

"I have found that to be God's own truth, my lady," he confessed, thankful that it was so, for how could he wish to bring to wife someone who courted predictability?

* * * *

After Melisande had changed for the noontime events, she made her way to the table and benches out on the east lawn where the guests chatted away, waiting for Helena. White canopies had been stretched overhead to provide shade.

Helena appeared, looking as beautiful and regal as ever. Everyone stood, as if she were a queen. At that moment, Melisande was proud to know Helena and counted herself lucky to hold such favor in the lady's company.

"Ah, Lady Bergavny." One of the men offered her his seat at the table.

"My thanks, Sir Riley," Helena said to the gentleman, and he handed her down to the bench.

The meal was served and pleasant conversation accompanied it. Not long after, Helena cleared her throat, gaining the attention of everyone present. "Now, Melisande, I realize this day is to be the end of our time together here at Willowbrook and I cannot bear to see you return to that lonely castle all by yourself. Would you consider staying on with us for a sennight or so?"

Melisande glanced around at the other guests. Their faces conveyed a friendly sort of envy at hearing Lady Bergavny's personal invitation to her.

Helena then added, "I wish to visit London in two days hence, and your company would indeed mean quite a lot to me. 'Tis but a three hour ride from here when the roads are dry. I pray thee, say you will."

"My lady, I would be honored to stay on at Willowbrook, thank you." *Argh!* Melisande nearly clapped her hand over her mouth. She had not thought before she spoke then remembered Devin. Staying on at Willowbrook would mean battling her lust for him night and day. She looked down at what was left of her bread and cheese, and could not eat another bite.

* * * *

As the sun dipped below the hills on the horizon, the Bergavnys bade farewell to a few of their guests. Melisande wandered the grounds of Willowbrook alone. No one seemed to notice her climbing the stairs to the battlements, so she continued exploring. She ran her hands along the rough stone parapets.

She came to a tower that connected the pathways and stepped into the room. The torches in the inner room had been lit and as she stood bewildered as to who would have left them so, musical instruments began to play just beyond the arch at the opposite end of the tower. Devin appeared through the doorway and strode toward her. She smiled, realizing he had done this for her.

Devin stopped in the center of the small room and placed his hand over his heart. "You are like the stars…and your voice is as lovely as…the wind and…your eyes are pools of…gray…"

Melisande stood silently for a moment. She dared not laugh, for she knew how difficult this must have been for him and was deeply touched. The wall of ice she'd built around her heart melted at his awkward attempt at romantic prose and her resolve ebbed away. If she had not fallen for him before this, she would certainly have given herself to him now. *'Tis no ordinary man who would go to this length to impress a woman.*

His hand dropped to his side, clearly declaring his ode at an end.

"Did you write that yourself?" Melisande asked, barely holding her mirth in check.

"I am sorry. I have never professed to be a poet." He grinned and placed his hands behind his back.

"Nay, forsooth 'twas…lovely."

At the same moment, they broke into melodious laughter that drowned out the lute and lyre. Looking toward the archway, Devin dismissed the musicians with a wave of his hand and turned back toward Melisande.

Her being flooded with a warm and overwhelming joy. Giddily she asked, "How did you know I was—"

"I did not. I do, however, confess that I'd pondered long and hard as to how I would entice you to this tower."

There was no helping herself. She reached up and threw her arms around his neck as high as she could. Devin in turn pulled her close.

"Your efforts are the sweetest thing a man has done for me in all of my life," she said, and briefly touched her forehead to his chin.

"Your late husband never recited verse for you?"

Melisande attempted to stifle a giggle. "Nay not, and by the by, how did you find out I was widowed?"

"I hear talk," he replied, tossing his head to the side in dismissal of the subject.

"And what else did you hear?"

Devin's smile faded, his eyes turned deep green and the torchlight reflected in them. "I also heard that you have not been with a man since he died," he said in a low voice, slowly leaning his face toward hers.

Melisande's heart pounded as it always did when he was this close.

"Remind me to dismiss those two gossiping maids from my employ," she said half-heartedly, tilting her chin up. Their lips brushed together so lightly it tickled. Devin's tongue gently teased her lower lip and her body melted along with her legs out from under her. She felt his arms tighten around her, keeping her from falling.

So much for her sainthood. The short-lived battle for her widowed purity was forever lost. And now that she was resigned to that fact, she no longer cared. *And so what? 'Tis not as if I am relinquishing my virginity.* She hadn't realized until this moment how lonely she had been. *It feels so wonderful to be in Devin's big, strong arms. This is heaven.* She pulled away enough to sigh and murmur, "What is it about you that makes my mind bemused?"

He answered her silently with a kiss.

With each passing moment, his embrace became more intense as they melted closer together and lovingly feasted upon each other.

Melisande wanted more of his tongue.

He stopped kissing her and growled playfully. "Will you eat me alive, then, woman?" He reached down, his hands cupping her bottom, and pulled her toward him until she was flush against his hardness. "I would like that." And he began again with his plundering kisses.

She could barely reach the floor with her toes. "Devin…" came her ragged groan as he nipped her cheeks then her neck.

"Aye, Melisande. You will be mine," he whispered.

He was fire, he was sustenance—he was the very air around her. She wanted him to make love to her. Right now.

As if she'd said it aloud, Devin lowered them to their knees. She tugged at the belt around his tunic as he peeled her robe from her shoulders. He was sucking and licking her neck and lifting her skirts at the same time. She needed this—needed him—and would do anything to feel him inside her. She stopped fussing with his belt and hefted her skirts, exposing her bare thighs.

Of a sudden, there were footfalls approaching from one of the paths.

"Melisande. Are you up here?"

It was as if a bucket of cold water had been poured over their heads. They stood up and Devin quickly tugged Melisande's robe back over her shoulders.

"Is that you, Helena?" Melisande answered shakily, making certain that her hem fell to where it ought to have been.

"Aye. Where are you?"

Melisande started to walk forward and Devin grabbed her gently by the waist and pulled her back to his front. "Stand here, love," he said next to her ear.

Melisande nodded in response to Devin's plea and spoke to Helena again. "In the tower."

"Oh, there you —" Helena paused, and for the briefest of moments, gaped at them, then recovered. "I am sorry. I have done it again, have I not?"

"You have done naught, Helena," she said, trying to comfort her hostess.

Melisande glanced up at Devin. He simply smiled at Helena, but said nothing.

Helena dropped her head and spoke to the ground. "I only wanted to inform you that supper was being served in the main hall, but really, there is no need to rush."

"I for one am starving. And yourself, Devin?"

"Aye... *Starving*."

"Devin!" Melisande said softly, with a hint of a giggle in her voice. She brought her arm back and abruptly elbowed Devin in the ribs. She sobered and continued, "We shall join you straightaway, Helena."

Melisande started forward, but could yet feel Devin's warmth as he tarried close behind.

Chapter Eight

As the trio passed the staircase in the main hall, Melisande excused herself to change her robe, which had gotten soiled somehow.

Devin spoke to Helena in a low voice. "At this time, I would be once again in your debt if you would refrain from informing Melisande about my knighthood."

"What? I do not think I understand—" Helena said, her brows pinched together in puzzlement.

"I fear I have not fully won the lady's heart as of yet, you see, and, well... It is difficult to explain."

Helena smiled. "Do not concern yourself, young man. I shall keep your secret for now," she murmured as they approached the dais.

Melisande joined them at the table moments later. Her new robe was of a deeper green than her gown and was lined with white fur. Devin considered that he was dreaming as he looked upon her, so lovely was she.

Supper's attendance consisted of the Bergavnys, Melisande and Devin, an intimate, cozy gathering. *Not unlike a real family*, he mused, more at ease than he'd been in some time. In contrast to his contentment,

Melisande ate and drank as if she was about to be executed and this was her last meal. Devin observed her ravenous appetite as if to ascertain the reasoning. It was unthinkable to him that their meeting in the tower would have upset her overmuch. *After all, nothing happened,* he thought with a twinge of discontent. If he could have, he would have taken her that instant from the room to his chamber and given her such physical pleasure she'd never have wanted to leave his bed.

Several times Lord Bergavny tried to make conversation with Devin, but he kept getting cut off by Helena, thank the heavens. He would have given away Devin's secret for certain. Melisande likely noticed nothing unusual about the behavior at the table, as she was on her third goblet of wine and second game hen.

After supper had been cleared, conversations went on around Melisande as she listened half-heartedly to the murmurings of the people in the room. She'd folded her hands tightly in her lap while she wondered at her reckless behavior and hoped that the fires of hell did not yawn before her. *Why does this man bewitch me so? When he steps into the room, everything I have been taught about propriety flies out of my head, as birds fly out of a pie that had not the proper time to bake. If any other woman were in this situation, would she feel the same way? He is more thoughtful than any man I've known. Why, his wit and charm alone melt down any and all of my defenses. I really shouldn't...*

Melisande glanced over at Devin, who had been watching her from across the room for nearly the entire meal. From over the top of his wine goblet, he stared at her as if in a trance. Melisande could not help but return his gaze. *Aye,* she thought, *any woman would be helplessly lost and at the mercy of his penetrating eyes.* Devin made her feel alive, desirable. He wanted her, and it had such a stirring effect as if it would topple the hills themselves.

"Would you not agree, Lady Dupree?" Lord Bergavny's voice penetrated Melisande's thoughts.

Melisande turned to him, having no idea of what he was speaking. "Aye, most definitely, my lord," she said with a demure smile then turned to Helena, who was sitting to his right. "I am ready to go to my room, Helena. Will you escort me?" she asked quietly.

Helena looked at Devin and back at Melisande. "Mayhaps Devin would see to that task for me this eve."

She would have swooned had there been Helena's companions present, but mercifully, the Bergavnys and Devin were the only witnesses to the exchange. Melisande's mouth fell open as horrified disbelief overcame her.

"Helena, my dove" — Melisande heard Fitzherbert softly address his wife — "would that be proper? I mean, after all — "

Helena leaned closer to his ear and whispered something no one else heard. Fitzherbert's face turned red and a great, wide smile spread across the expanse. "Very well then, you are both excused for the evening," he declared.

Melisande flushed, imagining the juicy bit of gossip Helena had just presented to her husband. She couldn't believe any of this. She started to stand and Devin was instantaneously next to her, offering her his arm. She accepted the help only to steady herself she avowed as they headed for the stairs.

"Sleep well, my dear," Helena bade.

Devin glanced over his shoulder and Fitzherbert winked at him. Devin grinned and reached up to wave back in acknowledgment.

Melisande tugged on Devin's arm to gain his attention. "Can you think about what this must look like, Devin?"

"Nay, forsooth, I am thinking about what it shall look like the moment I get you alone."

"Devin! Where is the seriousness of the matter?" Melisande scolded with a harsh whisper. "We mustn't depart in such an obvious manner."

"Pray, my lady, why should you be ill at ease? These are dear friends we've just supped with, not pious priests."

Melisande refused to believe that Helena and her husband would condone this sort of behavior in their home. Helena could have at least provided an excuse for Melisande, as opposed to helping her into a large basket headed straight for the fiery lake.

They reached the top of the stairs. "You go toward the stairs to your chambers and I shall go to mine and we will say our good evens from there," Melisande suggested.

"You can't be serious." Devin chuckled aloud.

"Shh…" She looked over her shoulder and down the hall. "Just do this one thing for me," she pleaded.

"And how shall you repay me?"

She didn't need to be a scholar to know exactly what he wanted. Embarrassed, Melisande directed her gaze to the ground. "I can think of no way."

Devin's voice changed from mirth to a low calm. "Then allow me. Come to me this night." He lifted her chin with his knuckle so he could look into her eyes. "You know how much we both want this."

"Nay. Truly. I-I mustn't," she whispered, shaking her head.

Devin's finger traced a path down her throat. "Melisande, I desire you as I do no other, and can see that you want me as well."

Melisande closed her eyes for a moment, his warm words heating her being. "Very well." The response seemed to escape her lips in quiet surrender without her even trying.

Devin considered her for a short moment then a look of pleased surprise appeared upon his face. "How long?"

"Just wait for me," she answered, her gaze once again lowering to the stone floor.

"Please, make haste, for I cannot bear much more of this torture." He took Melisande's hand and raised it to his lips, brushing a kiss across her knuckles.

They reached their doors, and from across the corridor, as if she were making a pronouncement, Melisande said, "Gramercy, Devin."

Devin shook his head, smiled and returned in his rich, deep voice, "Goodnight then, Lady Melisande."

At the bottom of the stairs in the great hall, Helena and Fitzherbert covered their laughter with their fingertips.

"You, wife, are the devil's own helper."

"Nay not, my lord. Oft new love must needs be encouraged—as a mother sparrow nudges her chick from the nest."

He took her hand, pulled her over onto his lap and buried his face in her neck. "Come, wench," he murmured. "Let us retire from this room, and find a quiet spot to remember what it was like when we were young lovers."

"Oh, Fitzherbert!" Helena giggled.

* * * *

Melisande ordered a basin of scented water to her room, and had Maggie coil and secure a braid at the top of her head. When the wash water arrived, she dismissed the girls and used a good portion of the perfumed French soap, a luxury item she'd like to have a wagonload of.

Satisfied, she made good use of the drying cloth, then slipped her arms through a thin white robe, deliberately excluding her chemise. A shiver of delight trickled up her spine at the thought of her scandalous behavior. And yet, as she snuffed out her candle and lay down upon the bed, her stomach flip-flopped with embarrassment. Pushing her whirling thoughts aside, she closed her eyes and waited for the household to settle in for the night.

* * * *

Melisande gasped and sat up. How long had she been asleep? Her tardiness must be a sign from above. *Mayhaps I should not go.* She swung her legs over the side of the bed, hoping to clear her thoughts, then after a moment, stepped barefoot onto the rush-covered floor and remembered her state of undress. Wrapping the flimsy fabric tighter around her body, she bound it with a long white hair ribbon about her waist so that it held fast.

After deciding to not wear her soft leather slippers in case they made too much noise, she crossed the floor of her room. She paused as she wondered at how her thoughts flitted about, as if her mind was attempting to discredit the task before her.

The indecisiveness she was experiencing was enough to make a person run mad. Her mind would say one thing and her heart would echo contradictorily. In fact, ever since she'd met Devin it had been this way. It was as if Melisande was caught between two worlds and they were both trying to tell her what to do. Was she the only person in all of England who battled with their own wits?

Melisande paused just inside her door, about to change her mind yet again, when she remembered something. She had given her word to Devin. Melisande placed her knuckles on her forehead and paced toward her bed and back again. *What to do! What to do!*

What if she just looked in on him, and if he were asleep, she could unkiss the agreement and say that she too had fallen asleep?

That was it. Her decision was now set in stone.

Melisande pulled on the heavy oak door and peered out into the passage.

Empty.

Taking little notice of the cold flagstone against the bottom of her feet, she felt her breathing draw in then rush back out of her lungs so loudly that she was sure it echoed down the corridor. With every step she took, she pictured how he looked at her, how his hands felt on her body, his enticing male scent. Melisande started to shake. Was she cold or was she frightened that he might still be awake?

At his door, she took a deep breath and silently pushed it open just enough to slip through. By the light of a single candle, he looked to be asleep. Relief and disappointment clashed within her as if they were engaged in an intense wrestling match out on the lists. She began to back out of the room.

"Melisande?" Devin called to her softly from the bed.

"Aye?" her barely audible voice escaped from her throat.

"I pray you, enter."

Mercy, how I want to. And yet, I'm afraid. I wish for a glimpse of heaven and run at the first sight of it.

Just being in the same room with him made her want to feel his body pressed against hers. It was a much easier decision when he was absent from her sight. Or was it?

I long to be touched by his strong hands.

If only someone else would make the decision for her, someone quite removed from the situation.

"Come to me." Devin's voice sounded gentle but urgent.

Again she felt the now familiar yet extraordinary pull toward him. At once the voices and warring emotions ceased, leaving behind the fading sounds of words unspoken. Arriving at the conclusion that her heart had won the debate, Melisande closed the door behind her and started toward his bed.

She wanted him. God forgive her, but she wanted him. She was no silly virgin. Pretending to be so would be a mockery.

Melisande ascended the two steps at the foot of the bed as if in a trance and looked at Devin for a moment. She then untied her robe and let it fall away.

Devin's gaze caressed her and he held out his hand to her. "Never have I desired a woman this much in my entire life."

His whispered sentiment left a mark upon her heart. Not in a million years would she forget his words. She climbed up, took his hand, and knelt on the bed before him. Devin sat up to share her position and Melisande pressed herself against him, suddenly embarrassed by her uncovered body.

A low chuckle rumbled in his throat and he proceeded to uncoil the braid from atop her head.

Once her hair was down and falling over her shoulders and breasts, Melisande lifted her hands to brush the stray hairs from her face. Devin pulled back from her just enough to get a long glimpse of her bare chest. Soon after, his hands followed where his gaze had been.

Melisande could no longer wait to touch him. She explored his thickly muscled torso and arms with her hands, in awe over the strength of him. His young, tight body was a new and wondrous experience for her.

In silence, they touched, kissed and nibbled by the light of the candle, exploring each other, memorizing, worshiping. The soft kisses Devin placed over her chest, shoulders and neck made Melisande quiver as desire lanced through to her very soul. He was so gentle with her, timid even, and yet it seemed he knew exactly what he was doing, making her feel cherished and adored.

She lightly scratched her nails down the back of his head, her hands buried in his soft golden-brown hair. Devin blazed a hot trail with his mouth across her cheek until their lips met, and at the same time, his hand skimmed over her hip and across her belly while the other rested on the small of her back. When his fingers threaded through the curls at the juncture of her thighs, she drew in a shuddering breath and exhaled Devin's name, urging him on. Clutching at his shoulders to steady herself, she found them rock-hard, yet warm, adding to the thrill of his closeness.

His hand slid lower, his touch almost tickling, then he nudged between her folds with such skill she found she could barely breathe. Each caress seemed like she'd never experienced such a thing before. Applying more pressure at her back, he held her captive between his vise-like hands. Her head lolled back as he teased her opening, barely inching a digit inside then out to skim the flesh once again, his rhythm never faltering. She sensed a frenzy begin deep within her belly, like heavy rain clouds threatening to drench the land.

He withdrew his fingers and it felt as if he'd ripped her from slumber. "Don't stop," she pleaded. "Touch me there again, in that same way."

He did as she had bidden. "You like it when I stroke you between your legs, don't you?"

Her shameless panting answered for her, the pressure building beneath his play.

"It makes you wet, readies you for my cock."

At his words she cried out, her fingers digging into his shoulders. Like a storm her climax was — fierce, unrelenting — and she wished it would never stop. Her hips strained forward, succumbing to this new magic he'd drawn from her.

Still on his knees, Devin lowered them both to the bed so that he lay atop her. His skin was almost hot to the touch, his length covered her, enveloped her. She complied readily when he coaxed her knees apart.

His cock slid over the soaked flesh between her legs, teasing her again the way he had with his fingers, circling, almost entering but pulling back. She thrust her hips forward, begging him to slip inside.

"Are you ready for me, wench?"

"Aye," she sighed, very near another climax. "Make haste lest I expire from wanting you."

At last his cock penetrated her, filling her completely. She felt stretched, ready to burst and teeming with the most luxurious sensation. In and out he stroked, her hips following his cadence. Her body buzzed like the wings of a hummingbird, her muscles strained under the weight of his body, reaching for more. With her arms wrapped around his neck and his tantalizing invasion insistent, stroking, caressing, she knew their spirits had melded together somehow. He took her higher than she had ever been with Liam, and her lusty cries seemed only to encourage him.

Devin's actions became insistent. Melisande tried to meet him halfway, but he was in complete control, so she wrapped her legs around him, glorying in the strength of him. Melisande's world shattered as Devin drove into the depths of her soul. Just when she thought she could take no more of his body's demands, Devin continued to deliver to her his sweet violence, causing her to climax again. Once the waves subsided, he finally poured forth a sigh that was more a growl. His body shuddered.

Finally spent, he rested his weight on top of her. She felt utterly surrounded by this beautiful man and never wanted to leave the blissful plane.

Devin finally pushed himself up only to look down at Melisande. His expression was that of wonderment. She wanted to ask what he was thinking but leaned up and kissed his sweat-dampened chest instead. He disengaged and positioned himself next to her. Falling back onto the pillow, he gazed at her. Melisande returned his look and saw yet another fire starting in his eyes. *Liam may have been a great warrior, but a more splendid lover will never be found than this man.*

Chapter Nine

Melisande shyly smiled up at him and his heart sank in his chest. He took her grin as an invitation for him to ravish her once more.

Devin made love to her, slowly this time, worshiping her body, revealing in her the multiple layers of passion he knew she'd suppressed for so long owing to her widowhood. Neither of them required time to recover in between climaxes and he wondered at the fact that it had never before been like this for him. It was Melisande who drove him and he wanted to give her all. And he did, until a cock crowed in the distance, warning the earth of the impending sunrise.

Finally, he recognized the deep breathing of sleep. He set his gaze upon Melisande, and saw that she was smiling as she slept. The realization hit him that it was he who had created within her this contented disposition. Devin tucked the bed sheet tightly around them and nuzzled her neck, inhaling her womanly scent. He knew life could not be better than this. However, it was not to last beyond a few more minutes, as the household would rouse at any moment. Had they been man and wife, they could have stayed in bed for a week and no one would have been able to draw them out.

"Melisande, love." Devin tried to rouse her, but she just lay there, deep in her slumber.

She stirred. He felt a bolt of hope. However, she merely rolled over.

"It is essential that you wake now," he said, the hint of a taunting melody in his voice.

"I do not want to," she responded as she pulled the thin coverlet over her head.

"You must." Devin tried to peek at her.

"Nay, let me sleep," she ordered, and snatched at the corner of the sheet he'd lifted.

Devin chuckled. "You, my lady, are a very difficult person to awaken come the morrow's dim light. Why, the castle could have fallen down around us and you'd *still* be abed."

Melisande sighed heavily, as if annoyed with the insistent voice that nagged at her while she was trying to sleep.

"You can't be angry at me. You need to be found in your own chamber come the dawn."

Melisande slowly slid the covering from her face and opened her eyes. "Devin," she sighed.

The sound of his lover's thoroughly feminine voice nearly stole the breath from his chest. "Tempt me not with your beauteous voice, my sweet nymph." He pulled her up to a seated position and held up the gauzy robe she had so deliciously slid away from her skin at the foot of his bed mere hours ago.

"Come now, you must retire to your own chamber or you will need to have a very good story for those maids of yours."

Melisande rolled her gaze to the rafters and back, then stuck her arms through the sleeves of the robe. Devin helped her down from the bed. "Go now to your room. 'Tis nearly dawn."

"Devin, my legs ache," she complained, yet half asleep as he climbed back up to his bed.

Devin smiled, pleased with the effect that his lovemaking had left with her. "Fine then, stay if you wish. I do not care what people will say when they find you in my bed," he said, reclining back onto his pillow, interlocking his fingers behind his head as if he didn't care a whit.

"All right. I am going," she replied, clutching her robe shut.

"Will I see you downstairs to break our fasts?" he called to her.

"Not before I sleep more." She shut the door behind her, weakly shuffling down the hall to her room, glancing hither and thither for persons who might espy her sluggish flight.

After she had pulled a fresh chemise over her head, Melisande slipped between her coverlets.

What seemed like moments later, Maggie and Tilly bounded into the room, and one of them threw aside the tapestry so that the sunlight practically set the place afire.

"Good day, m'lady."

"'Tis time to rise and break your fast."

She covered her eyes with her hands, the light having caused a searing head pain. "How is it that you two are so cheerful in the morning?" she grumbled in the direction of her maids.

"We are happy that we are to be staying on at Willowbrook, my lady," Maggie chirped.

"So up you go. The day shan't wait!" Tilly continued. "I have chosen your rose houppelande gown for today."

"Oh, very well." Squinting, she dragged herself to a seated position and wagged her finger at the girls. "However, I will not be wearing a hat—and I will brook no arguments over the matter, either."

"A braid then," Tilly announced.

"I shall fetch the matching ribbons," Maggie offered.

"No braid," Melisande said firmly.

"But, m'lady!" Tilly implored.

"Nay, I shall wear my hair down. Most, if not all, of Lord and Lady Bergavnys' guests have left and I wish to be more comfortable. That is the end of this conversation."

Thanks be to God they complied and stopped pestering her about it.

* * * *

Melisande made it down to the great hall before the tables were cleared. She found Devin sitting next to Helena speaking quietly. She cleared her throat politely and interrupted. "Good morrow, Lady Helena."

"Ah, good day to you, Melisande. How did you sleep last eventide?"

"I tossed about in the bed most of the night." Melisande had chosen her words accurately, but hid the humor behind a sincere countenance. It was her turn to speak boldly and put Devin at a loss.

"As did I, Lady Helena," Devin added as he rose from his chair and studied Melisande's reaction, as if in challenge. Apparently he thought he could not be outdone in jests.

"Greetings, Devin."

He nodded a bow. "Lady Dupree." Devin pulled out a chair for her on the opposite side of Helena. As he took her elbow, he pressed the white ribbon she had discarded at the foot of his bed last night into her hand. He whispered close to her ear, "Again." Devin returned to his seat, his gaze never straying from hers.

Melisande was glad to be seated, as she would surely have swooned at the remembrance. In return, her look penetrated back to Devin as if she were speaking to him without words.

"Well." Helena seeped into their private moment. "I must see to some tasks for today, so if you will excuse me. Melisande. Devin."

Devin jumped up and offered Helena his arm just as she began to withdraw from her chair.

"Do not forget about our trip to London on the morrow, Melisande." Helena left the hall in a swirl of richly embroidered robes.

When the mistress of Willowbrook was out of sight, Devin rushed to Melisande's side and knelt on one knee. Taking her hand in his, he kissed her palm. "I cannot bear to be away from you even for a few hours," he said against her hand.

"Nor I from you." She reached out and held his face, giving his jaw and cheek a tender caress.

"Would you ride with me this day, out farther into the countryside?"

"I would like that very much," she replied, removing her hands from him and folding them demurely into her lap. "What shall we do when we get there?" Her question hung in the air, filled with mock innocence.

Following their lusty romp not hours ago, her jest didn't go unnoticed. A low chuckle rumbled in his throat. "I have several ideas," he said, grinning.

Melisande leaned down close to Devin's ear. "I have some ideas as well," she said, breathing her words the way he had last night.

A wave of joy washed over Devin. He alone had brought out the devil in the angel before him and it pleased him to no end. He nuzzled her cheek and spoke softly next to her ear. "Not being a very patient man when it comes to these matters, I may not be able to wait that long."

Melisande shivered with pleasure, then pulled back just enough to gaze into his eyes. "You'd best be gentle. I can barely walk as it is."

"Hm. Then I must finish off the task properly."

Melisande giggled.

* * * *

Melisande and her lover spent the morning in and around Willowbrook, finding private corners to steal a kiss here, a touch there, and even a place to make hurried, passionate love before they were caught. To her this was heaven. She couldn't even remember what her life had been like before Devin.

At one point, Devin had dozed off in the grass behind a garden wall with Melisande by his side. When he'd awakened, he'd found that she'd placed tiny flowers in his hair, and some more were sticking out of his tunic and the tops of his hose. Melisande tried to flee from the 'two-headed posy monster', but he caught her, and pulling the flowers from his person, he stuffed them down the front of her dress, ignoring her giggling protests. Then, after kissing her until she couldn't remember her own name, he lowered them to the ground, shoved her skirts up to her waist and gave her a wicked pounding—the most glorious, soul-shattering sex of her life.

Even for the sake of propriety she was unable to cease grinning like the village idiot.

"I'm famished," he'd remarked after a while.

"'Tis no wonder, after all that activity."

He rolled over and pulled her to him. "I blame you, thou temptress."

Melisande giggled.

"Let us make for the great hall to find sustenance."

It was at that moment that she realized just how stiff her bones were, owing to his amorous attentions. Though it pained her to do so, she asked for assistance not only to help her recover from her recumbent position, but in addition, she begged his arm to lean on as they walked along.

And oh, how her smug lover bragged. She feared she'd never hear the end of it, which was fine with her as she never wanted the reason for his posturing to stop.

* * * *

After the noon meal, Melisande felt her strength return. Devin had planned for them to go riding, and she could hardly contain her eagerness. She had Tilly and Maggie dress her in something more appropriate in which she could more comfortably ride. They chose her soft blue, lightweight robes, intricately embroidered with dark blue birds of prey and flowers and a short riding cape in a rich cornflower with white rabbit fur lining. A matching chaperon had a wide pouch of lace netting in which to catch Melisande's hair. Her maids insisted on the hat for the ride. They commented that the hues of the outfit made her eyes seem very bright azure as opposed to their usual dull gray, which she thought perfectly fit her disposition after the morning's vigorous activities. Her reflection in a large, framed polished silver pane showed that her cheeks echoed the glow of love that had bloomed within her breast.

For the first time in her life, she felt utterly alive.

She came upon Devin already at the stables waiting for her. He wore a long, dark gray tunic over his tight, white, long-sleeved tabard, which emphasized his muscular arms. A thick silver belt sat about his slim hips, and tight white hose covered his powerful upper legs. His tall black riding boots shone like new in the light of the afternoon sun.

"Ready for our ride?" he asked, his smile as devastating as ever.

"I am. And what a blessing to have such a handsome man to accompany me." Melisande's gaze took him in once again. She observed the black panther's head on his tunic—it seemed familiar somehow, but she couldn't recall why.

Devin helped Melisande onto her side-saddle, then mounted his steed. "Come. I wager your pretty little mare, Guinevere, can keep up with Hector's strides." Devin and Hector took off at full gallop. Melisande sat staring for a moment, feeling slightly left out.

"Well, Guinevere, it's just you and me now." She clicked her gentle mount into a trot.

After she reached the first bend, she observed Devin riding back toward her, approaching at full stride.

He brought Hector to a halt next to Guinevere. "Pray forgive me." He sounded out of breath. "I did not realize how little you ride."

"Thank you for your consideration, Devin," she said, attempting to sound sardonic, but she couldn't hold back the humor that surely shone in her eyes.

"Teasing me, are you?" He tisked. "Such impudence." He leaned down and kissed her on the mouth, teasing her tongue with his. All too soon he pulled away, leaving her quite unsatisfied.

He grinned, obviously understanding that which her ersatz pout revealed. "Let us reach our destination and mayhaps we will finish this."

"Mayhaps?"

Devin chuckled. "Saucy wench."

They headed south for a short time and Devin led them into a dense copse of trees that provided protection from prying eyes. In the center was a grassy area large enough to accommodate the horses.

Surrounded by a thick hedge, Devin and Melisande lay down, facing each other in the grass. Melisande inhaled deeply of the fresh air. The sound of many birds flitting here and about and chirping happily made her feel relaxed enough that she could take a nap. However, when she looked at Devin, the vision that came to her was far too sweet to pass up. She'd ask him to take his clothes off then she'd strip down for him. They could then ravish each other and be like two beasts in the wild. Could she ask him for such a thing? Would it be terribly unladylike?

Much to Melisande's disenchantment, Devin spoke first. "I have wanted to ask you something, Melisande."

"What is it?" She leaned up on her elbow, inquisitiveness taking the place of her lusty idea.

Devin gazed at her for a moment. He drew a labored breath and continued, "What think you of the Willowbrook games?"

The Willowbrook games was not a choice topic, for certain. That was a question she would have expected from Liam, not this gentle lover she now looked upon with curiosity. She watched his face, trying to read his thoughts. She could not understand what this particular subject had to do with them.

"The truth," he added.

Melisande decided to share her innermost thoughts with him. Why, she had shared everything else with him, beginning last night. She adjusted her position to lie fully next to him then laid her head to rest atop her folded arm and sighed. "Devin, this is something that pleases me naught to speak of, but you did ask." Preparing for the unpleasant task of telling a true tale from her own life, Melisande became uncomfortable, so she sat up, placed her hands in her lap, and stared off into the distance.

"My late husband was knight to Lord Herbert Lancaster. We were married shortly after he retired from serving the noble, yet all he spoke of were the great battles he fought in, the weapons, the bloodsport..."

Devin shrugged and started to speak, but her next words halted him.

"There is more. He was old, aye, but he was also a ruthless man. Please do not think he was *always* that way—he never struck me... Well, not intentionally—"

Devin sat up, his abrupt action interrupting her tale. "Intentionally? I do not understand. You were but a child," Devin stated, indignation in his voice.

"Liam threw things. He pushed, he shouted— 'Twas as if he had...fits of rage. If everything did not go his way, whether it was the serfs or the crops, he would become very angry."

"'Angry' seems to be a mild way of describing such a disposition," Devin said, obviously perturbed. "How could a man—much less a knight—treat you with anything but reverence and respect?"

Melisande looked down at her folded hands for a moment. Familiar emotions overwhelmed her, filling her eyes with tears. "His rage frightened me. However, 'twas his right to treat me thus, for I was his wife." Devin opened his mouth to protest, when Melisande ended her account. "I have never told anyone this."

It took a moment for Devin to respond. "The weight of your situation must have been difficult to endure," he said, his voice tremulous with emotion.

Melisande nodded.

Devin moved to sit next to her and placed his arm protectively around her shoulders.

"'Tis why I do not like hostilities of any kind, be it mock battles or otherwise. I never wish to be part or party to that sort of vice ever again." She dabbed at the salty droplets that threatened to fall from her eyes with her sleeves.

Devin moved, this time to sit before her. "Not all knights are this way—most especially the more honorable men of the brotherhood."

"I have yet to meet a knight who does not continually talk of swords and killing…"

"Aye, you have indeed, Melisande."

Chapter Ten

"Of whom do you speak?" Melisande looked to him for his answer.

From inside his tunic, Devin pulled out a single red rose with a dark gray ribbon tied in a bow around its stem and handed the flower to her.

"I do not understand. What does a rose have to do with—" With a start she recognized the ribbon and remembered the championing of the knight at the joust.

The realization hit her like a blow to the stomach.

She drew a tremulous breath. "*You* are the Black Knight?" Her voice faltered, barely a whisper. She stared at him for a few long, painful moments, her jaw slack with astonishment. The rose in Melisande's hand began to shake. Schooling her tremors, she felt her features turn to granite.

Devin's words came out in a rush. "Melisande, I observed your countenance during the matches. I knew something had bothered you. I decided not to tell you—"

She interrupted him. "You. *Decided?*"

"Melisande, I never meant to betray—"

"Had I but known of... I would *never* have given myself... The things we did! Why, I let you—" A sob escaped from Melisande. Appalled at her behavior and sickened by his deception, she covered her mouth with her free hand. Tears began to flow from her eyes as the situation stabbed her heart like a thousand thorns.

"Melisande, please—" He raised his hands palm up to her in silent supplication.

A voice came from off in the distance. "Sir Devin? Sir Devin!"

Melisande stood up and took a few steps in the opposite direction of the voice, trying in vain to pat dry the tears that continued to fall from her lashes.

"Who calls?" Devin demanded.

"'Tis I, Parker, my lord." His young squire came running around the hedge.

"What is it?"

Parker was out of breath from running. "'Tis Sir Frederick. He needs your assistance. A *York*," the young man spat the label, "is trying to seize his lands from the north."

Devin could hardly believe what he was hearing. "Without any regard at all to the alliance between the houses of Tudor and his own York?"

"To this rogue, it matters not," Parker announced with indignation.

"Have you gathered my suit and weapons?"

"Aye, my lord. All is ready for the journey save for thee."

"I will go now." He took a few bounding steps toward his horse but stopped dead in his tracks when he saw Melisande's little mare grazing with his mighty stallion. Devin shook inside as he turned to face Melisande.

She stood there, her teeth clenched, her gaze hard.

"Melisande—" Devin implored.

"You lied to me."

She spoke with an intense force, as if her words were individual statements. She did this, he had noticed, when attempting to keep her anger in check. The echo hung in the air like a gloomy mist, but before Devin could defend himself she continued.

"Now go. Kill and destroy. I will not be at Willowbrook upon your return, that is, if you *do* return." Her voice cracked, bespeaking the vehement storm of emotion seething within her. "I never want to set eyes on you again."

"Melisande, Sir Frederick is my ally. I was but a page at the battle of Bosworth and Sir Frederick saved my life. I *must* go."

"Just leave me and let me wallow in my sins." She choked out her words.

"And what about *my* sins—I participated with you!"

"Do not speak of *that* again. You, *Sir* Devin, have no soul." Her full-bodied voice roared in his ears and echoed through his body. She glanced down at the rose in her hand and hurled it at the ground before him.

Devin withstood her rage, allowing it to pierce his heart. *I deserve this.* His scheme had failed, and, in turn, he had failed her.

Parker interrupted the scene impatiently from behind Devin. "Pray forgive me, but we must leave soon, my lord, for nightfall is nearly upon us."

Devin broke out of the intense gaze held between himself and Melisande and spoke to Parker. "See to it that the lady arrives at Willowbrook safely, for she will not allow me to reason with her at present."

"Aye, my lord." Parker nodded.

"Catch me up directly. I shall take the north road." Devin never looked back at her as he mounted his horse and raced off for Willowbrook.

"M'lady." Parker motioned toward her mount.

Melisande lifted her chin a notch or two before she spoke to Parker. "They have succeeded in turning you into one of them, have they not? Poor child." She strode past the boy and, stepping on to a low, sturdy branch, mounted her little mare without assistance.

She cried silently along the way. The only evidence of her torment was the constant stream of tears that trickled down her cheeks.

Chastising herself over and over again, she knew her penance would not only include multiple prayers offered to God, but her heart, it seemed, had been diced into small pieces, and the recovery, she imagined, wouldn't be forthcoming any time soon.

She allowed Guinevere to set a slow pace back to Willowbrook — taking Parker's silence as gratitude for the tempo of the ride, for he was still on foot.

* * * *

At Willowbrook, Devin had readily slipped into his armor with the help of a page and had prepared Hector with the saddle and dressings used for battle. After a brief conversation with Lady Helena, and with his sword at his side, he was on his way in just over a quarter of an hour.

He paused at the gates, steering Hector around so that he could gaze upon Willowbrook one last time.

"I will find you again, my Lady Dupree. And when I do, I shall convince you that our fates are intertwined. For better or for worse."

Hector pawed at the ground, seeming just as anxious to arrive at the approaching battle as Devin.

Forcing himself to focus on what lay ahead, Devin turned Hector back toward the road, giving him as much rein as he required. Propelling them forward, Hector's strides devoured the path before them.

* * * *

Melisande, for once, was thankful for her nosy maids. She sent them to search out fresh water so she could be alone to think, figuring they would take their time and visit with others along the way. One side of her felt a keen disappointment that Devin was gone. Yet, on the other hand, she was glad. She had naught to say to the errant Black Knight.

At first she tried to keep her mind occupied, but every time she relaxed she thought of Devin. Upon her maids' return, she had Tilly fetch her *psaltery* and instructed them not to call her to supper. In an empty solar at the southern-most end of the castle, Melisande made harsh the tunes she so loved to play. The composers of the beautiful songs, were they to hear the damage she was doing, would have splintered her instrument to pieces and bade her to never play again.

After some time, the anger within took its toll and managed to exhaust her. To be void of *any* emotion, she imagined, would be better than seething. She went back to her chamber and lay down upon her bed still fully clothed, save for her hat and shoes. She buried her face in her pillows and, unable to stem the tide, cried herself to sleep.

* * * *

The morning light brought with it the ever chipper Maggie and Tilly.

Pushing aside the tapestry and opening the shutters, Maggie exclaimed, "What a beautiful day for an outing with Lady Bergavny!"

"London. I am perfectly envious!" Tilly chimed in.

The maids chattered back and forth as they removed the rumpled gown that Melisande had slept in. They apologized profusely for not having been ready for her upon her early retirement. Just as Melisande could take their banter no longer, there was a knock at the door.

"Melisande, might I enter? 'Tis Helena."

Melisande looked up toward the heavens to implore God to get her out of this morning's activities, not that she felt she deserved His divine intervention. With a sigh, she called out, "Aye, Helena, you may."

"Come, let us be off the moment you are dressed. The sooner we get to London the better. I am anticipating a wonderful trip."

Melisande sighed. "Helena, I am afraid I will not be accompanying you on this outing."

Maggie and Tilly gasped and stared open-mouthed. Melisande shot her maids a contemptuous look and dismissed them with a wave of her hand.

The moment they were gone Helena sat down on the side of the bed. Melisande joined her there.

"Why, dearest?"

"I am not up to a journey to London or anywhere else this day, except mayhaps back to Dupree."

Helena took her hand, which Melisande reluctantly allowed. "Does this, perchance, have anything to do with Devin?"

The lady's directness took Melisande aback. "Nay. Aye. I know not. My companionship would be most ill-tempered this day, 'tis all."

"Child. Devin will be back in a twinkling and this trip will cause your mind to not dwell on thoughts of him."

Uncomfortable with the subject at hand, Melisande shifted upon the mattress. "What you need to understand is that it matters naught to me if *Sir* Devin ever comes back. I shan't be seeing him again." At her statement, Melisande observed guilt wash over Helena's face like a veil.

So, Lady Helena knew Devin was a knight and didn't tell me. Was it an oversight or did she hide the truth on purpose? She'd have to decide later whether or not to be upset with Helena.

"Melisande, Sir Devin is in love with you."

The simple statement took a moment to sink in. *Impossible. Love has many guises. Helena must be mistaken.* "Love? Ha. I think not. Lust, more like."

"Yesterday when Sir Devin came to me in a rush just after your outing he enquired, *'Where is Melisande?'* I teased him. *'Have you had a lovers quarrel so soon?'*

"In brief, Devin explained to me what he was about and that he had equipped his stallion for battle. I could see the anguish in his eyes and I am most positive it was because he had to leave you."

"He did not *have* to leave!" Melisande raised her voice then, failing to mask her emotions.

"There is no need to upset yourself. Sir Devin is a loyal man — loyal to his friends as well as to his loved ones."

There was naught she could do when tears spilled down her cheeks. "If Devin and I were to be together, *I* would have come first, *not* his bloody battles."

Helena put her arm around Melisande's shoulders and gave her a squeeze. "Above all, 'tis I who understand not being first in my husband's life, 'tis every woman's fate who falls in love with a knight of the realm. However, maturity brings with it patience, and the ability to see that there are many sides to love. I do not expect you to completely grasp the idea this very moment, but someday you will."

She pulled away from Helena and mopped at her tears with her sleeves. When Helena spoke again, her tone was much lighter.

"Now, my dear, if you are so determined to put Sir Devin out of your mind, this outing is just the thing. Fitzherbert left early this morn and is already in London visiting King Henry. They fought at Bosworth together with Sir Liam, if you recall, and Fitzherbert and Sir Liam were among the first to vow their loyalties to Henry when Richard fell."

"Aye, I remember the telling of that battle, many times over," Melisande replied, unable to prevent the subtly sarcastic tone in her voice.

"So now we go. Cheer up, young lady, for we have a grand day ahead of us." Helena nodded with mock seriousness.

By Helena's making the situation seem not so tedious, a diminutive smile parted Melisande's lips. Helena had been nothing but kind to her, with the exception of withholding Devin's title from her. She supposed Helena hadn't meant to hurt her. Melisande heaved a sigh, deciding that she couldn't be angry with Helena.

She nodded. "Very well, Helena."

Helena left the room, calling to Melisande's maids to finish dressing their mistress.

Maggie and Tilly selected a rich burgundy velvet robe to go over her rose-colored tunic. The matching veils were long and sheer with large, faceted amethyst stones dotting the headband.

The ladies boarded the wagon straightaway and took cheese, bread and fruit to eat along the way.

"I'm delighted you've attended me. I've not journeyed to London since last spring," Helena commented lightheartedly in between delicate nibbles of her cheese.

Melisande's only remarks were on the weather and the fare before them. She did her best to avert her thoughts of Devin's safety. *Why, he does not even deserve a single sentence of the Lord's Prayer said on his behalf because of how he deceived me.* And she dismissed the vision of his twinkling green eyes and devastating smile from her mind.

When the meal was finished, the constant motion and noise from the wheels lulled Melisande to sleep.

What seemed to her like moments later, the driver cleared his throat loudly so as to gain their attention. "M'lady, we shall be arriving at the first stop on your tour shortly."

"Thank you, Ian," Helena said as the two ladies did their best to smooth out their surcoats.

A fabric shop, which specialized in imports, was only the first of many shops down the long main thoroughfare. The streets were filthy to say the least and Melisande wondered at the thought of living so close to countless people. True, a good many inhabitants lived in and around Dupree. However, one could still find a place to be alone if one truly desired. Liam had told her of London a few times, but of these things, including the waste that was tossed into the streets and the odors that the debris emitted, she'd had no idea.

Helena purchased what seemed like yards of expensive embroidered fabrics, soft shiny materials and bolts of wool from France in a variety of colors. Farther down the thoroughfare she was measured by a dressmaker and ordered three gowns to be made for her.

"My maid Mabel's eyes are failing her of late," she confided in Melisande in hushed tones. "She only does light mending for me now."

Melisande had to admit, it was very kind of Helena to treat her servant so gently.

To the back of the dressmaker's storeroom, Melisande saw a deep cream-colored gown with gold wire embroidery throughout the garment that made it glow like the stars on a warm summer's night. When the pattern that had been sewn onto the fabric caught the light from the flickering candles of the otherwise dark little shop, it caused the dress to wink at her. It had a low neckline that was bordered by the same gold thread and sleeves long and wide with white short fur around the cuffs. Its arched bodice was so heavily decorated with gold beads and pearls that it would have been fit for a queen. The headpiece that hung on a peg protruding from the wall nearby had a thin band of the same white fur of the cuffs and a short length of fine gold chain mail that hung down the back that was long enough to reach the nape of one's neck.

"Helena, have you ever seen such beautiful craftsmanship?" Melisande asked as she stroked the fabric.

Helena gained the attention of the head seamstress. "What of that gown in the corner?"

"'Tis been here nigh over a fortnight now. The *lady* who ordered the thing be made decided against it," the woman said with no small amount of spite. To say that she was unhappy with the person who had not picked up or paid for the expensive garment would have been a grand misstatement.

Helena nodded to the woman and whispered to Melisande, "'Twould be a most comely gown worn by you. But do not let on that you are interested. The shopkeeper might overhear and come up with an outrageous price."

"On what occasion would I wear it, were I to acquire it?" Melisande asked, turning from the beautiful gown to face Helena.

"My dear, when one shops, one also makes purchases for future events, whether known to one or not," Helena stated with an air of mystery in her voice.

"Besides, I fear I did not bring a purse of coins or other means to make purchases," Melisande confessed.

"Permit me to make this purchase for you and mayhaps at a later date—"

"But you and Lord Bergavny have done so much for me these past three days, I could not ask you to—"

"You did not ask, Melisande, I offered and insist that you agree," Helena whispered, her tone motherly.

Melisande looked back at the artistry of the dress and sighed. "It is lovely, is it not?"

"'Tis settled then." Helena turned toward the shopkeeper to haggle over a price while Melisande caressed the stiff threads of the design with her fingers.

"Sold." Helena dismissed the woman, turned back to Melisande and smiled. "I had expected to pay twice what she originally offered," Helena whispered. "I brought the price down by another third. I should have been a merchant." She chuckled.

When the woman returned, Helena called Melisande over. "Have Lady Dupree measured and the gold dress altered to her specifications. If the project can be finished quickly, there will be a few extra coins for you."

"Aye, my lady." The gray-haired woman bobbed a curtsy to Helena, then shoved aside a curtain. "There's work to be done here. Quit your gossiping of the King's Garter and get to thy needles," she called out to the young girls under her employ.

Melisande was somewhat excited about the new gown, but her actions still lacked fervor owing to the brief visions of Devin that she had to continually dismiss from her mind.

Helena and Melisande left the women to their work. Halfway through the portal of the next shop, Ian hailed them. "Pray forgive me, m'lady," he said, trying to catch his breath from the run across the thoroughfare. "I just come from speaking with a messenger of the King's who came upon your conveyance with m'self aboard. It seems that Lord Bergavny has told our good king that you and your talented young guest are about town this day. The King requests yours and the Lady Dupree's presence for supper tonight at his Royal Majesty's high table."

"Thank you, Ian. That is the best news we have heard all day. Is that not right, Melisande?" Lady Helena sounded elated.

"Grand," Melisande said rather flatly, though she didn't mean to show her displeasure. Her preference remained to be at Dupree, alone with her thoughts.

"Ian." Helena tossed her driver a coin. "Go pay a visit to that pub across the way and meet us after you have quenched your thirst."

The man grinned and tipped his hat, which bore the colors of Willowbrook. "Oh, gramercy, Lady Bergavny. An' God save yer ladyship," he said with a tip of his cap and a sincere smile.

In each shop the two ladies visited, Lady Helena had to let everyone know about Melisande's personal invitation from King Henry. The shopkeepers were so impressed that they practically gave away remnants of sheer chiffon cloths, satin ribbons and shiny trimmings to Melisande and Helena, hoping that they would wear their items before His Majesty.

Later, Ian loaded the last of the ladies' packages onto the wagon, which he had picked up from along the route.

"I'll be toppled over if the horses make it all the way to Windsor Castle, let alone to Willowbrook," Ian half jested.

"Which reminds me, Ian, you will need to make two more trips to the tailor's shop. One on the morrow for a purchase made for Melisande and one in two days hence for my goods."

Ian stole a sideways glance at Lady Helena and asked, "Pray tell, m'lady, does Lord Bergavny know of yer purchases?"

"Not as of yet, Ian. I do, though, hope he is sitting when he finds out!"

As she listened to their tinkling laughter, it occurred to her how kind Lord and Lady Bergavny were, even to their serfs. In such grand yet humble company, Melisande at once became eager to arrive at Windsor, and to experience court for the first time.

They drove along the Thames for quite a while. Lady Helena allowed Melisande the window with the view of the river, having seen it many times herself. When they finally reached the gates of Windsor, Melisande wished she could ride up top with Ian.

They alighted from the wagon and Melisande was in awe. Windsor Castle was massive in comparison to Dupree or even Willowbrook. The palace guards stood like statues, not looking one way or the other. Helena and Melisande marveled at the grand structure from the center of the courtyard.

Melisande was to be presented to King Henry just before supper, so she and Helena refreshed themselves in Lord Bergavny's guest chambers.

As the ladies were conversing about the grounds, the décor of the room and the King himself, Melisande felt the excitement mounting and only thought of Devin once, when she wished that he would be by her side when she met King Henry. She pictured him escorting her down a long stretch of polished marble to where the King sat on a bejeweled chair. In her vision, Melisande looked up at Devin only to find him in his full suit of armor, holding a bloody sword.

Melisande walked over to the gleaming brass washbasin and splashed the clear, cool water onto her face as if to rinse away the daydream. She resigned herself to the fact that Devin was a long way from London, and had not been invited to come. Even if he were to suddenly arrive, she reminded herself, she would have nothing to do with the knight.

Chapter Eleven

Melisande's newly gained elation reached a fevered peak moments before she and Helena were announced as she saw Lord Bergavny at King Henry's right, their heads together in conversation. As she and Helena approached the dais, the King and Lord Bergavny stood. He must have held the Bergavnys in high regard for His Majesty to have done so.

"Your Majesty, may I once again present my wife, the Lady Helena Bergavny."

"Your Most Royal Majesty." Helena bowed her head and executed a flawless curtsy that nearly left her prostrate on the ground.

"Pray recover, Lady Helena. It seems like only yesterday when you and Lord Bergavny were at the festival of All Souls we held here at Windsor," the King said, reaching for her hand.

"A wonderful time was had by both Lord Bergavny and myself at the festival, Your Majesty," Helena replied sweetly as her fingers slipped into his palm.

"And may we say you look lovely as usual," he said in earnest.

"I thank you, Your Highness, for the generosity of your compliment. Now may I present to you the Lady Melisande Dupree, a most talented young woman and a dear friend." Helena stepped aside and indicated Melisande.

Melisande emulated the curtsy Helena had moments ago offered the King. "I am honored to make your acquaintance, Your Most Royal Majesty."

"Recover and come here, my child."

Melisande stepped forward and stood within arm's reach of him. She felt an odd surge of pride to be so close to the King and kept her gaze reverently diverted from his.

"Lord Bergavny has told us that you are widow to Sir Liam Dupree. He was one of the finest knights we've ever had the honor of fighting by our side." The King paused. "Forgive us, Lady Dupree, for that was a long time ago. How have *you* been faring?"

Melisande knew King Henry was a peace-loving man. She admired the fact that he'd taken a bride of his family's enemy in order to end the civil wars that had been continuous for over thirty years. "I have been very well, Your Highness. The Lord and Lady Bergavny have helped me through my grief a tremendous amount of late."

"Good, good," the King replied genuinely. "Now, my dear, we are very much in the mood for a fresh musician to play for the court this eve following our repast. We oft grow tired of the selections that make up the litany of our royal musicians." He chuckled. "Mayhaps you will teach them some recent pieces to play for us."

"I will do so to the best of my abilities. I am your humble servant." Melisande curtsied again.

"Excellent. Now, let us sup together at our table."

Elizabeth Stuart of York, now Queen Elizabeth Tudor since her marriage to the King, joined them at the high table. Melisande was then presented to her and found her most gracious.

Along with the Queen was a relative of hers by the name of Corin Sinclair.

Upon her introduction to Corin, he took Melisande by the hand and brushed his lips just below her knuckles, at the juncture where her fingers met. "M'lady, if you are half as talented as you are beautiful, we are in for quite a treat."

Melisande's cheeks heated and she felt a strange fluttering of her insides at the handsome visage before her. "Gramercy." She hoped she didn't sound like the village idiot. She couldn't think of a single phrase witty enough with which to rejoin him.

Corin was tall and solidly built, one could tell by the cut of his richly embroidered tunic, for he had wide shoulders and a broad chest that tapered to slim hips. The warm color of his eyes resembled a rich, creamy brown that could melt a woman's heart at twenty paces. He had smooth, glowing skin that would certainly make the most beautiful *femmes à la cour* jealous. His smile revealed straight teeth that were as white as virgin snow. His hair was just a tad darker than Devin's... *And almost as long,* she mused, finding herself comparing the two men. Nearly in the same instant, she chastised herself. *Melisande, stop dwelling on things that cannot be.* Then again, how could it have been her fault? *'Tis the Black Knave who invades my thoughts, and at the most inopportune moments.* Melisande painfully pushed Devin to the back of her mind and smiled up at Corin Sinclair who, for some reason, still held her hand.

"Your eyes hold such immense expression, my lady," he commented as he helped her to her seat.

Apparently, his courtly manners dictated that he not comment directly on what had surely shown on her face. Perhaps someday she would learn to mask her thoughts so as not to be so transparent.

Melisande enjoyed cheerful conversation with Corin and the other courtiers over an eight-course meal—which was by far more food than Melisande had ever seen in her life at one table.

Not long after the grand sustenance had settled in her stomach, the servants cleared away the tables for the evening's entertainment. King Henry called for his musicians to begin playing in the minstrels' gallery.

The royal musicians performed a few pieces from their repertoire by rote, while three jugglers delighted the crowd with their skills. Balls, silver plates and all manner of objects were tossed high into the air and passed back and forth between the brightly clad men. Even when whetted swords were flung to and fro before the gathering, the men seemed heedless of the danger. As the whirling blades finally came to a rest in the deft hands of the three performers, Melisande expelled the breath she'd held, waiting for blood to be spilled all over the King's floor.

When the applause dwindled to a minimum, the King turned to Melisande. "Lady Dupree, if you would take your place amongst our musicians, you may begin for us the demonstration of your aptitude."

Melisande crossed before the King and curtsied. She continued on to the stairs of the gallery and took the stool at the clavichord, bidding the musicians to listen then join in.

She began the piece, and as the lovely music filled the room, she saw that the King was pleased, for his eyes were closed and upon his face he wore a grin. The musicians around her nodded to the rhythm and slowly, one by one, added harmonies that complemented the melody.

At one point she observed Corin Sinclair speaking with Helena. Melisande made note to ask Helena what he'd said to her.

When the music ended, Melisande made her way down the stairs of the loft. She curtsied to King Henry and his queen, Corin and Lord and Lady Bergavny. Henry stood and descended the few steps to stand before Melisande.

Taking her hands and speaking personally with her, not in his royal plural, he stated, "That was lovely, my dear. The familiarity of it puzzles me, for I must have heard that piece in my dreams."

'Twas common enough. However, she felt she must proceed with caution. Any sort of instruction may offend the King and make her look as if she were being defiant to his majesty. This was indeed the last thing she wanted to do. Her gaze remained diverted from his, and she spoke as gently as possible "'Tis a standard piece oft taught to budding musicians, and it is said to be popular amongst bards throughout Europe. I am most certain you have heard the tune at one time or another, though possibly presented in a different way."

"But how? When?"

"I assume you have had a fair share of singing troupes to entertain you at court?"

"Of course," the King replied. He reached out and tipped her chin up.

She met his gaze with as much bravery as she could muster. "'Twas but an Italian madrigal set with music instead of voice."

The King thought for a moment, and the grin that registered on his face caused his eyes to shine with joy. "I remember a group of singers that came not long ago. They did in fact speak and sing in Italian, and, if I recall correctly, they sang that very song without any instruments."

"Precisely. A madrigal is a song without instrument save for vocal intonations," Melisande gently instructed.

The King looked into her eyes and spoke aloud, "Most astonishing, Lady Dupree. The King is indeed diverted."

Melisande's very being heated at the compliment. "Not just I, 'twas your royal musicians who remembered the piece as well."

King Henry straightened and in a proud voice proclaimed, "Your grace and humility greatly please this court." A burst of applause rang out and Henry bent down to whisper in Melisande's ear, "You are a breath of spring air, Lady Dupree."

A dainty laugh escaped from between Melisande's smiling lips and she kissed the King soundly on his cheek. "I thank you, Your Majesty."

Henry returned to his chair, his face ruddy from the exchange.

Queen Elizabeth patted his hand. "The granddaughter you would like to have someday?"

"Most definitely." Then he turned back to Melisande. "Go, sweet lady, refresh thyself and join us directly."

"Aye, Your Majesty." She curtsied low to the King and Queen then made her way across the room and out of the door to the royal gardens.

Henry motioned for his musicians to begin playing again, and Corin positioned himself between the King and his cousin, Queen Elizabeth.

"I am of the thought that Lady Dupree is most talented," Corin commented so that only Henry and Elizabeth could hear.

"Quite," Elizabeth agreed.

"Aye," Henry replied. "We would be indeed fortunate to have a lovely and skilled musician such as Lady Dupree in our midst."

"Exceedingly fortunate, your Majesty." Corin agreed and continued. "Lady Dupree is a widow, is that not correct?" He enquired, already knowing the answer from his conversation with Lady Bergavny.

Elizabeth leaned forward to look beyond Corin to her husband, cocking an eyebrow at the King.

Corin observed the reaction, then watched as Henry raised both his brows in silent communication to his wife. "When we granted Castle Dupree to Sir Liam, we were well aware that it was well positioned and possessed fertile fields."

Suppressing a chuckle, Corin mused, *Aye. Both Dupree's fields and their lady are fertile.*

Elizabeth addressed Corin. "What is it you are hinting at, my dear cousin?"

Corin merely smiled and returned to a more comfortable seated position. *What a boon to have the lady of Castle Dupree right here in our midst. Almost effortlessly, my plans are moving forward.*

Melisande reappeared and sat next to Lady Bergavny. Helena patted her on the knee to indicate that she was pleased with Melisande's playing. Melisande placed her hand atop her elder's and gave it a gentle squeeze, silently thanking Helena.

"I saw you in a private moment with Corin during the entertainment. Of what did you speak?" Melisande whispered to Helena.

Helena shrugged. "I hardly remember. 'Twas nothing of note."

Puzzled at Helena's nonchalance, Melisande settled back against her cushioned chair. Surely Helena had no reason to dislike Corin Sinclair.

She sat quietly and listened to the blend of music and murmurings of the people as they conversed, when, after a time, Corin approached her, bending at the waist as he addressed her.

"I wanted to tell you personally how very much I enjoyed your playing earlier," he expressed to her as if in confidence, his lips nearly making contact with her cheek.

Melisande couldn't help but smile and, wanting to know more about this exquisite male, turned to look him boldly in the eyes. "I thank you, Sir Sinclair," she stated, hoping the title of 'sir' did not accompany his name.

He responded with a deep chuckle as he stood up straight. "Alas, I will never have the honor of being knighted. I am afraid I am too comfortable with the life of leisure I lead here with my cousin at court."

Melisande was relieved and slightly embarrassed by her misjudgment. She tried to recover her blunder. "Forgive me, Mr. Sinclair, you…have the build of a knight—I mean, you have a look about you— What I am trying to say is—"

He obviously enjoyed the flattery she was spilling all over him, for this time it shone on *his* face.

At long last, he tactfully ended her sputtering. "I want you to call me Corin," he said with a sincere smile then continued, "Now it is my turn to thank you by offering one so lovely as yourself some wine." He reached out and softly stroked the back of her hand with his fingers, as if he sensed her flustered emotions and wished to soothe them.

Grateful that this fine young man had so gently defused the foolish scene she was making, she permitted him to fetch for her a goblet of the King's malmsey. "Again, thank you, Corin." She was now of the opinion that Corin was most thoughtful, and took blissful pleasure in the attention he was giving her.

Corin found a servant carrying a tray of goblets with jewels encrusted around their circumference, and bade that the cups be filled to the rim. He observed the King's court jesters preparing to go on for the guests this eve. Corin got their attention and motioned for them to come to him. "Where is your third man?"

"We dismissed him, my lord," the performer called Shelby confided. "He was so bad at jollity that he added tragedy to our comedy," he said gravely then grinned at his own jest.

Corin made to enquire further—however, thought the wiser of it. "I want you and Bean"—he indicated Shelby's partner—"to do the magic rope trick that I saw you rehearsing yesterday, and I want Lady Dupree, the young woman in the burgundy robes who sits on the dais with the other honored guests, and myself as victims—I mean, volunteers," he amended. Tossing them each a coin, he then added, "And not a word about this to anyone."

Chapter Twelve

Corin rejoined the group at the dais, stood next to Melisande's chair, and handed her a richly embellished goblet filled with wine. "Lady Melisande, you shall not find a sweeter potion in all England." Then he added in a lowered voice so that only Melisande could hear, "But I believe I have found a lady who is even more agreeable than the taste."

Melisande thought her cheeks would never lose the heat they had acquired this eve. "Corin, you are being—"

"Too forward? Pray forgive me," he murmured, leaning in closer still.

"Nay. I wished to say 'too kind'." She admired his beautiful face. However, her gaze lingered a moment too long. Now *she* was being forward. *The second a man pleasing to look upon gives me a compliment, I melt like beeswax long-exposed to the elements on a bright summer's day.*

Melisande's thoughts were distracted by the entrance of King Henry's court jesters. Corin promptly retreated to take a seat, much to her disappointment.

"Gather round one and all, for what we have to show you will confuse your mind and tease your eyes! I am Shelby and this is my assistant, Bean." Each of the colorfully dressed men took a bow. "Bean and I were in a village near the sea the other day, and do you know what we saw?" A few of the people in the audience shook their heads, but Bean nodded.

Shelby looked at Bean and, rather annoyed, stated, "I know *you* know. *You* were there."

Bean merely shrugged.

It was obvious to Melisande by the dull look in Bean's eyes that he was not a very bright fellow.

Shelby continued, "We saw a man on the ground kneeling and bowing toward the east. The shocking part came when he sat up, for we could tell that he was obviously not one of King Henry's subjects."

Bean snapped out of the daze he seemed to be in and yelled, "A spy! A spy!" and proceeded to run around frantically in a small circle. His voice was wobbly and high-pitched and it made Melisande giggle.

Shelby calmly removed his hat and with it gave Bean a swat on the arm to settle him down. "He was not a spy, you ignorant fool," Shelby said, replacing his hat.

"Oh, pardon," Bean said, coming to stand once again next to Shelby.

"Now where was I?" He shot his partner another stern look and continued. "When he came out of his trance, he stood and looked right at us."

"For sooth, right at us," Bean encouraged.

With a vexed look on his face, Shelby turned his head slowly to face Bean. "*I* am telling the tale, imbecile."

"Pardon," Bean said apologetically. The onlookers chuckled.

Sighing, Shelby continued, "It was then that the little man actually spoke to us. '*My prayers have been answered,'* he said. *'You will purchase from me my rope for six silver coins. You will acquire the magic rope, and I shall not go hungry.'* We were an answer to his prayers, what choice did we have?" Shelby implored of the crowd.

"Verily, what could we do?" Bean said, mimicking the tone of Shelby's voice.

Shelby's hat swung once again at Bean, but this time he ducked out of the way. The unsatisfied Shelby hauled off and gave Bean a swift kick in the shin.

"Ow! That 'urts!" Bean howled as he brought his knee up to his chest. He hopped around on his good leg as the court chuckled heartily.

"Oh shut up, you moronic excuse of a— Oh never mind, you are not worth the trouble. Now, be quiet and show our patient audience what we purchased from the small man."

Bean patted down his clothing as if looking for something on his person. "Oh indeed, I remember where I put it." Bean removed his belt and tossed the front of his tunic over his shoulder. His thigh-length, bright green, full-sleeved tabard and multicolored hose were the only garments now showing.

"Well, where is it?" Shelby said impatiently.

Bean reached under his tabard and pulled out, from what looked like his loins, the end of a rope. Taking it in both hands before him, he paused and looked out at the audience, and, with a wry grin, said, "Here it is!" he ground out lustily then winked at the audience.

The crowd's shoulders shook with mirth as they tried to keep their eyes on the insolent Bean.

Bean proceeded to pull out the rope little by little and his face took on an extremely smug look as if he were the proud owner of the longest 'rope' anyone had ever seen.

Everyone in the great hall roared with laughter and King Henry mopped the tears from his eyes with the sleeve of his royal robes.

Shelby's impatience overcame him and he glowered at Bean. "You are taking entirely too long. I am sure the King has much more important things to do than watch you pull on your rope."

Shelby and Bean's audience were now doubled over with hysteria.

On his last nerve, Shelby exclaimed, "Oh, give me that thing!" He grabbed the rope and with one swift yank removed the rest of the rope from Bean's undergarment.

"Ouch!" Bean yelped. "Be gentle with me!" he finished coyly, batting his eyelashes.

The audience was now holding their sides and stomachs, gasping for air while battling fits of laughter.

Shelby started gathering the rest of the rope off the ground. "Go make yourself useful and choose two volunteers to participate in the magic."

With another shrug of his shoulders, Bean walked over to the crowd and right away chose Melisande. "You, m'lady, will do nicely, and…you, sir, come with me." Melisande looked up as Bean took her hand to lead her down the steps, and saw that it was Corin who was to be the other 'volunteer'.

Bean placed Melisande and Corin back to back in the center of their impromptu theater in the round, directly in front of the King and Queen.

"Nay, nay, thou witless, blundering slob, not that way!" Shelby said while coiling the rope.

Bean turned their shoulders so that they were facing the spectators. Melisande wished fruitlessly that all the torches and candles in the room would get snuffed out simultaneously. She was not at all bashful in front of an audience, but only when *she* was in control of the entertainment.

"Oh, can you do aught right?" Shelby shouted at Bean as he handed the neatly coiled rope to him. Shelby turned the couple face to face, or, rather, Melisande's face to Corin's chest. "My, you're a big one!" Shelby said to Corin. The audience gave up a roar of laughter.

Melisande eyed Helena. It seemed she was displeased, if the scowl on her face told aught. Instead of joining in with the merriment, she merely shifted in her seat. *What could have vexed her so?*

"Hold this here—" Bean said as he handed her one end of the rope near her upper arm. "And put your other hand here." Bean had her place her hand on Corin's shoulder. "Now please place your feet in between the gentleman's feet." Melisande helplessly did as she was told. "Very good," Bean said to her as if talking to a child. Melisande could not look up at Corin's face. She stared at his green velvet tabard with gold embroidery instead.

"You, sir, will you place your hands like so?" Bean positioned Corin's hands on Melisande's waist. Melisande glanced briefly at the audience and everyone was smiling and hooting… Except for Helena.

Bean started circling the couple with the rope, round and round and round until the other end of the rope was at their ankles.

Shelby turned to Bean and asked irritably with his hands on his hips, "Now, how are we to tie the ends, Bean? You oaf!"

"Sorry," Bean said and retraced his footsteps backward, unwinding the rope all the way.

"Give me one of those ends, you imbecile. Remind me on the morrow to find a new partner with some sense about him," Shelby grumbled.

"Very well," Bean said obliviously.

Shelby's gaze swept across the high ceiling with much exaggeration over Bean's last remark. He placed Melisande's other hand on Corin's shoulder and pushed them even closer together so that they were flush against each other.

Melisande felt a moment of panic but shoved it to the back of her mind. She would endure this performance as the court had endured hers.

Shelby proceeded with the task that lay ahead of him by placing the center of the rope around Melisande's shoulders and across Corin's back.

Shelby addressed Bean. "Now take this end and wrap it around opposite the way I do." Shelby and Bean tightly circled their captives until they had enough rope left on the ends to tie a strong knot.

"Can you move all right?" Shelby asked the couple.

"No. Not a bit," Melisande replied, her voice muffled by Corin's chest.

"Good," Shelby said abruptly, ignoring her statement.

A hot flush worked its way up Melisande's face as the audience laughed. Suddenly in need of air, she turned her face to the side. If only she could catch his eye, she would glare at the performers. Mayhaps then they would quickly find the climax of their tale. "Now, Bean, where did you put the guidance parchment?"

"I do not have it, you do."

"Come now, Bean, the old man handed it to you—I distinctly recall it."

"Nay, I do not remember such a thing."

Shelby raised his voice then. "How are we supposed to complete this trick if we do not know *how*?"

"Do not look to me, 'tis no fault of mine," Bean said, raising his hands palm up in surrender.

Shelby removed his hat and gave chase to Bean, swinging at and missing his head all the way across the room and out through the doors that led to the gardens.

As the crowd applauded, Melisande finally raised her gaze to Corin's.

Corin shrugged and said, "Well, I suppose we are stuck here until Shelby and Bean can find that parchment." A surreptitious grin made the corners of his mouth curl up.

"How long will that take?" she enquired.

"I am not sure, but there are worse situations I could think of than this to be in. In fact, I am finding this quite tolerable," Corin said and flashed his perfect smile at her.

Melisande's pulse quickened and the room seemed to grow even warmer. She glanced around and remembered that she was tied indiscriminately to Corin. *One doesn't even dance as close as we now stand.* All at once in her mind's eye she saw Devin's face and remembered their dancing at Willowbrook.

Helena jumped from her seat and tried to untie the knot. "Fitzherbert, could you please assist me? I cannot seem to undo this."

"Oh, Helena, let the young people have a little fun," he replied, still chuckling.

"Fitzherbert. Please," Helena implored.

"As you wish, my love." Lord Bergavny stood, sobering some.

When they finally came unbound, Helena took Melisande by the hand, obviously forgetting about the King and Queen. "Come, Melisande, 'tis time we retired for the evening."

Because of her scandalous behavior before the court, whether innocent victim or not, Melisande complied immediately.

They had not ventured three steps when the Queen spoke to her hastily departing guests. "One moment, please, Lady Bergavny." Helena and Melisande stopped dead in their tracks and turned toward the dais. "Before you and Lady Dupree retire, the King — my husband — has an announcement." She indicated him with an upturned hand and a nod.

"Verily." Henry cleared his throat. "We would require that you stay at the palace for another day. The Queen and I are going to hold a masque, and it is our desire that you and the Bergavnys are present."

Melisande was in no way ready to attend a celebration so soon after the damage done to her heart by Devin. She turned to Helena and stepped closer for a private, hurried conversation. "Inasmuch as I would like to, I would rather not, Helena. I must be getting back to Dupree."

"Melisande, 'tis a rarity that the King offers an invitation to surprise guests such as ourselves. 'Twould be wise to stay."

"Helena, I have nothing to wear to a masquerade." Melisande's tone was pleading.

They both heard Fitzherbert clear his throat as if to tell them that they were taking too long in making a reply to their king.

"We shall have to improvise," Helena whispered in a rush. Their heads came up simultaneously, and Melisande knew her placating smile presented a none too authentic expression. "We would be honored, Your Majesty." Helena curtsied deeply and Melisande followed suit.

"Excellent," the Queen replied.

Still in the center of the room, Corin addressed Melisande. "So, I shall see you again at supper on the morrow's eve?" The question that hung in his languid, sensual gaze practically took her breath away.

Perhaps it is not such a bad idea to stay after all. Melisande nodded slowly, her heart pitter-patting erratic beats under his scrutiny. "Aye, Corin." She smiled prettily, vowing to scold herself later for being so horrendously fickle. She supposed that she would have plenty of time to mend her broken heart when this enforced holiday was over.

Corin closed the distance between them in four strides, took her hand and raised it to his lips. "Save the first dance for me?" he queried, then lingeringly kissed her hand.

Melisande basked in his courtly manners, her indecisive apprehension all but forgotten. "Most assuredly," she whispered.

"Come along, Melisande. We have much to attend to before the morrow." Helena pulled Melisande by the other arm.

"Until then," Corin said as Melisande's hand slipped from his.

Yet ensnared by Corin's hot stare, Melisande wiggled her fingers at him in a farewell gesture, and he in turn regally inclined his head toward her.

Chapter Thirteen

Helena threw open the shutters of Melisande's room and the bright morning light seeped between her closed eyelids. Up until this moment she'd lain asleep, peaceful and satisfied in her warm little nest.

"Melisande, the morn is half wasted. Ian has arrived with our packages and is now loading them into my chambers. Arise from thy slumber, my dear, we have several things to see to."

Melisande mumbled none too discreetly, "Will no one in Christendom let me sleep? If my maids aren't plaguing me 'tis someone else." Attempting to wipe the blurriness from her eyes with the heels of her hands, she continued, "Where is it written that we must get up with the cock?"

"You know the old proverb, 'early to bed, early to rise'," Helena said cheerfully.

"Well, as I recall" — Melisande yawned — "'twas but a suggestion."

She eyed Helena's smile at the quip and Melisande stretched like a cat underneath the pile of fabric.

"My lady, what is so important that you must drag me from one of my favorite pastimes?" Melisande sat up.

"Why, the masquerade this eve. Are you not excited?" Helena asked incredulously.

Recalling Corin's flirtations, Melisande looked down and pretended to study a tassel from one of the elaborately embroidered blankets that lay across her to conceal the sudden change in her attitude. Quickly reining in her nearly riotous feelings of enthusiasm, Melisande stated, "Oh, aye. 'Twill be pleasant."

"'Pleasant' is not the word *I* would choose. Wonderful, mayhaps splendid, but 'pleasant'? Merry child, 'tis your first gala at court, Melisande, should you not be *slightly* more jovial?"

Helena was obviously giddy with the approaching event, but for far different reasons than Melisande.

At once, Melisande unleashed the sparkling smile she had hidden from Helena a moment ago. "Is this more to your liking?" She was loath to mention that Corin was the cause of her delight.

"Much more, indeed." Helena nodded. Dropping the subject, she continued, "Now get up, for I need your assistance with my costume, and when that task is complete, we shall see to yours. There is some broth on the table next to your bed. Drink it down and come assist me."

Melisande climbed out of bed, donned the robe that was provided for her by the Windsor servants, and sipped on the warm broth.

* * * *

Helena stood in the center of the room so that Melisande could observe her from a better vantage point. "Oh, my lady, you have the look of a Greek goddess."

They had taken the bolt of material Ian had brought up and draped it over and around Helena's body. Melisande had secured the folds with a few strategically placed stitches and a leather belt at her waist. Her hair was pulled up to a taut bun and thin, silvery, metal leaves from the trimmings given to them by the shopkeepers were situated in her hair around her head as a crown. Helena took most of the leaves and formed them into a mask, leaving two holes for her eyes, and the rest she fashioned into the handle.

Later, Ian arrived with Melisande's gold gown and headpiece from the shop in London. She put the dress on and spun around. "This is truly the most delightful gown I have ever owned. Thank you again, Helena."

"You can thank me by turning the heads of all the young men at court this eve."

Melisande laughed aloud.

Helena studied Melisande for a moment and her cheeks heated under the lady's knowing gaze. "You seem to be in a more agreeable mood as our day progresses. What has employed you so?"

She smiled at Helena and swirled around again. "Do you think Corin will like my new gown?"

Helena's chin came up and she took an indignant stance. "That young man is too forward with you. Neither of us knows this Sinclair well enough to trust him. You mustn't be enchanted with those charms of his so easily." Her words poured forth, scolding Melisande as if she were a child.

"My Lady Helena, who was it that gave me the advice that I 'need to experience more of what life has to offer'?" Melisande said with her hands on her hips.

"You... You mustn't soil your reputation."

Melisande folded her arms across her chest. She had fared quite well without a mother for some time now and did not wish to be directed about like a pawn in a game of chess. "I do not have a reputation. What I have is a dead husband." Melisande fairly shouted the latter, but she couldn't help herself. *And when I think of the encouragement Helena gave me when Devin was pursuing me... Why, she practically tossed Devin and me into a room naked, and locked the door behind her.* She dared not speak her thoughts aloud. The last thing she needed was to shed more tears over the affair with Devin.

"Melisande, it is not good to speak of the dead so," Helena said, slightly more docile.

"Well, 'tis the truth," Melisande said and spun toward the window. *This is a most horrible conversation. I am finally beginning to enjoy life and now...*

Helena surrendered with a heavy sigh. "I suppose, in this circumstance, you are correct."

Melisande returned her gaze to Helena and nodded curtly.

"Make a promise to me and I shall not present this subject to you again."

"What promise is that?" Melisande asked flatly.

"Promise me you will not dance every dance with Corin this eve."

Melisande tried not to smile thinking of the handsome Corin Sinclair.

"Fair enough. I promise."

"I thank you." With that, the subject was tabled. Although for how long, Melisande knew not.

Mostly in silence they began to work, only speaking when presented with trivial things, which suited Melisande just fine. They examined the pile of trimmings and remnants they'd received from the fabric shops. Helena found a strip of thinly hammered metal, a swatch of gold satin fabric, long white ostrich feathers and small white, smooth-textured stones cut into halves. She called to one of the maids passing by in the hall to fetch needle and thread for her.

In no time at all, Helena had fashioned a mask for Melisande.

"I am afraid this mask is too heavy to attach to a holder," Melisande said as she tried to bend the rest of the metal into something that resembled a handle.

Helena looked at the mask and picked up the hat that matched the new gown. "Mayhaps we can remedy that."

Helena attached the mask to Melisande's headpiece, and when Melisande tried it on, Helena's invention fit perfectly.

By that time it was the dinner hour, but they were too exhausted to dress and join the other courtiers for the midday meal. Melisande suggested a nap for the both of them until it was time to make ready for the King's party. Helena agreed to the idea, and, after helping Melisande out of her golden gown, went to her own room.

Even though 'twas Melisande's desire to rest, she had a difficult time actually getting to sleep. Anticipatory about Corin, she kept thinking about how attractive he was and how gentle his touch had been on her waist, his elegant manners and chivalrous ways— *What is not to trust?*

Mere moments before slumber overtook her, her thoughts strayed to Devin.

* * * *

Melisande's hunger brought her groggily back to the living. Rising from her recumbent position, she realized she'd only had the broth earlier in the day. Curious as to where Helena was with Lord Bergavny's costume, she donned a simple robe with much haste. Later, there would be food in abundance at the King's table, she was certain.

Inside the Bergavnys' chambers, Melisande found that Helena was already dressed and had fashioned her husband a similar costume to hers. She sat quietly in a chair and observed the couple.

"This wisp of a skirt you have me in is rather drafty. Is there naught else I can wear this eve?" he complained gruffly.

"Nay, dearest. This is all we have to work with, and besides, if the wild clansmen of the north can go about bare bottomed in the out of doors all their lives in naught but a short woolen shroud, then you can survive for this one night with a draft nipping at your backside. 'Tis a wonder I have any of these items at all. Melisande and I were very fortunate to have obtained them."

Fitzherbert conceded with a chuckle. "Only for you, my love." He lifted a corner of the soft silk of his short costume and enquired of his wife, "By the way, where did you say you acquired these remnants?"

Melisande watched as Helena searched for a way to tell him just how successful her shopping tour had been, when a soft knock sounded at the door. In lieu of an answer for her husband, Helena quickly called out, "Enter!"

It seemed that the Queen had sent Helena and Melisande one of her ladies in waiting to attend to anything they would need to have done for the masque.

"My lord, it seems we will have to address this subject another time. Melisande and I have much to attend to before the masque." Without another word, Helena swept from the room and escorted them to Melisande's chamber. She instructed that the maid help Melisande into her gown, and also what to do with Lady Dupree's hair.

Helena had the Queen's lady braid and coil Melisande's hair so that it did not show under the short length of gold mesh attached to her headpiece. When Helena finally departed, the woman proceeded to fuss over every other detail until Melisande had a mind to run mad over the anticipation of it all.

Melisande sat impatiently at the ready. Just when she could no longer stand the wait, Lord and Lady Bergavny ventured into her room. "I understand that Helena is also responsible for your costume."

"Indeed. She has been most kind." Relieved at their visit, Melisande stood and turned in a circle to show off Helena's accomplishment.

He held out his hands to Melisande and declared, "You look like divinity ensconced in gold, my dear," he said as she placed her hands into his elderly ones.

"Gramercy, Lord Bergavny," Melisande said as she placed a chaste kiss on his cheek.

"Let us be off. I am famished!" Helena hurried them along.

* * * *

The great hall was alive with what seemed to Melisande over a hundred voices, each trying to speak over the music. When her eyes drank in the wondrous colors and textures of the courtiers' costumes, the whole picture felt like a living, breathing dream. Lord and Lady Bergavny were announced at the entrance to the room, as was Lady Dupree. One of the King's personal valets led them to the high table.

Everyone in the hall stood when King Henry, as a rather wealthy Robin Hood, and Queen Elizabeth, as a bejeweled Maid Marian, entered and took their seats. Then, without delay, steaming food was brought to the tables and course after course was put in front of the guests. Meats, from salted boar's head to oxtail, fowl from game hens to swan, shellfish and sugared mackerel, and cheeses that Melisande had never seen before served carved into various shapes. Different kinds of bread for dipping in rich sauces, or to be used for trenchers, and the malmsey flowing generously. Melisande's goblet was refilled many times.

She had wanted to taste everything even though the first course had been sufficient. When the desserts were presented and she had finished only half of her fruit tart with the thick honey glaze, Melisande could stand it no longer and pushed her chair away from the table. As she excused herself and began to stand, Corin was instantly at her side.

"Oh, good eventide to you, Corin." She reached out and gratefully took his strong arm, as she felt as if she fought for balance in a small boat on a stormy day. "I was just on my way out to the gardens for some fresh air, and here you are!" she said, her words slightly slurred, as if her tongue and lips weren't in agreeance with each other.

She smiled, thinking her belly must have been sloshing out loud with food and drink.

"May I escort you, Lady Dupree?"

"'Twould seem that we are in fact at that point already, Corin," she said with a slight giggle, then sobered immediately. "But really, I insist you call me Melisande."

"If you wish it," he replied.

As he led the way toward the doors, Melisande leaned most of her weight on him, confident in the fact that he was more than able to take it. Poor Corin nearly had to steer her as they went along — she could feel his grip tighten and loosen as she wove her way across the empty path. But, somehow, it didn't bother her in the least.

They walked into the courtyard of rosebushes, young willows and hedgerows that were themselves shaped like short-walled mazes, and stopped in front of a bench.

Corin broke the momentary silence. "Your headpiece is most fashionable for this masquerade, Melisande."

"Oh." She reached up. "You may have it then." Melisande began tugging at it, trying to remove it.

"Nay, forsooth, there is no need to disassemble your lovely costume, I was but admiring the originality of the combination of the hat and mask."

"'Twas Helena's idea. She created the mask and attached it to the band of fur." An unladylike hiccup escaped from Melisande. She grinned and covered her mouth briefly. "Pardon me," she murmured daintily.

"Truly, there is naught to excuse." Corin took her by the wrists and turned her so they were facing each other. With his voice lowered he enquired, "Tell me. Who is Helena?" His question sounded like a statement, as he flashed her one of his heavenly smiles.

Melisande, high from the effects of the rich food and wine, and his devastating looks not helping in the least, slid her hands up his chest, around his neck and pulled him down, slowly moving in for a kiss. "Why, Lady Bergavny, of course," she said on tiptoe and against his lips.

Corin did not respond to her answer but, she noticed, he was quite pleased to oblige her action.

At once she broke away from the kiss and marveled at her surroundings. Sighing a long and audible sigh, she said, "'Tis a most beautiful spot. Gardens and courtyards of late have been magical places for me." Melisande looked into his eyes and added, "What of your experiences, Corin?" She found her own boldness startling, but felt she had hidden this new revelation well.

"Magical. Now there is an interesting word, love. Any place you venture to can be made magical, providing there are the right circumstances," he said matter-of-factly, in that smooth, rich voice of his, all the while lowering them to a seated position upon a bench.

"What do you mean, for example?" she asked and moved closer to him, her thigh brushing against his.

He grinned. "Well, for instance, I could take you to the wall, walk up on the battlements under a full moon, and kiss you senseless."

Melisande sighed again and leaned her head on his thickly muscled upper arm. "Do go on."

He regarded her for a moment then continued. "I could take you to the royal stables, and toss you around in the hay like a common servant girl."

"Corin! You would not do such a thing!" she scolded with a smile, which she knew completely negated her reprimand.

"Mayhaps if you gave me the chance," he replied in a hushed voice, his grin blossoming to a full smile.

"For shame!" She slapped him playfully on the chest. Corin caught her hand and kissed each finger.

"Now tell me, what would you *really* do?" she purred.

He gazed out into the night sky. "After you have your bath, I will brush out your hair in front of the hearth until it is dry. Then I will carry you —"

Melisande pulled her hand from his grip, placing her finger over his lips. "Shhh... Listen, Corin. The rounds have begun."

"That is neither here nor there. Come now, let me—"

"Oh, but it is. I promised you the first dance!"

"'Tis unnecessary to—"

"Nay, I must keep my word. My honor is at stake." She nodded once to show her sincerity. "You understand, do you not?" She was unwilling to give him the opportunity to reply. Instead, she jumped up and pulled him off the bench and toward the sound of the music.

He mumbled to himself, something about two flagons of wine, but she dismissed it.

Now in the light of the torches and candles about the room, Melisande had a chance to really see Corin's costume for the first time. He wore bright blue from his pointed shoes to the feather in his cap. On all of his fingers he had rings of gold with sapphire stones of different shapes and sizes. *No outfit he could come up with could take away from his handsome features,* Melisande thought dreamily.

There were more attendants dancing than had been at supper. The costumes that the guests wore were rich in color as well as cost. Mock kings and queens, jesters, beasts, bandits and more were on the dance floor.

Melisande let the music take her away, body and soul. The turning and swirling currents of air felt cool against her skin. One dancing partner after another she teased and flirted with. She could not understand why she felt so deliciously free this eve, but it was so lovely to be so, she didn't care. Nor did it bother her that, for whatever reason, her steps felt less graceful than usual.

One of the costumed men she danced with, a Norseman of old, addressed her just above a whisper as they danced. "Be careful, little star, or you shall outshine the Queen herself." And he stepped away, leaving her with the next partner and her jaw hanging open in bewilderment.

It took a moment for his words to seep into Melisande's mind, and she blinked a few times at the tingling sensation he had caused. Melisande missed a few steps as a result of the expanding distance between them, and the mock king she was now dancing with asked if she needed assistance.

"Nay, all is well, sire," Melisande said to the man and smiled sweetly from under her mask.

Thinking that the song was more than half over, Melisande fretted over the fact that she and the Norseman might not cross again within the dance, for he was most intriguing. She searched for him across the crowded room and found him gazing in her direction, or so it seemed — his face was mostly concealed by the mask of cloth he wore, which protruded from beneath his hammered metal helmet.

Her fears were confirmed as the circular was at an end, and Melisande was ever so curious as to who this Norseman was. She started toward him, but of a sudden, the floor slanted, more so than it had been. It reeled and spun her off balance. Melisande reached for a bench by the door to the courtyard and held fast, but, alas, the entire room began to tilt wildly. She was instantly swept up by two strong arms and, just as her vision faded to black, she saw her Norseman hovering over her.

Chapter Fourteen

Melisande awoke and found herself in a dark corner of a hallway adjacent to the courtyard, still in the arms of the Norseman. She started to speak. "How long have I been—?"

"Not long, little star. You know, one must be careful with the King's wine, for this will be the result when one overindulges."

She protested. "I did not overindulge—" Melisande had to hold her hand to her forehead as her own words assaulted her frail condition.

"Had you more than two tankards full?" he asked, rather amused, as if already knowing the answer.

"For your own knowledge I had..." She paused trying to recall. "Ohhhhhh..." she groaned. "I remember not."

"Therein lies your answer." he replied insolently, as if she were a child.

This must look to him as if I am the town drunkard. Impatient to change the subject of her irresponsibility, her mind rushed to find a topic. "Why do you call me 'little star'?"

"Because you remind me of a star that has fallen from the night sky."

Melisande felt the heat in her cheeks and was thankful for her mask.

"What is your name?" Melisande asked.

"'Tis not necessary to know by what name I am called, for I am only passing through, just as you are," the Norseman replied mysteriously.

"But, how will I know you once we part company?"

"You may know me by my kiss."

"Mayhaps it is you who made a meal of the King's wine, or do you not recall? I have not kissed you," she announced with no small amount of choleric.

He nodded and exhaled in what seemed to be near surrender. "Very well, then. We shall wait here until you resolve to take a kiss from my lips."

The thought of kissing him, with his velvety voice, *did* fascinate her, but could she be so bold as to cast aside the fact that she had exchanged but a handful of words with this man? The scenario was awfully familiar. However, she could not place it, so she pushed the thought aside.

"I could not kiss you, what would you think of me?" she asked as she tried to shrug out of his heavy arms, which immediately strengthened their hold upon her.

"I wonder..." the Norseman thought out loud and glanced over his shoulder. "How long until the sun rises?" He looked back at Melisande. "With a lovely lady such as yourself in my arms, I may be persuaded to have the patience of Job."

"Oh, very well." Melisande didn't care to waste time arguing with him. She placed her hands on the sides of his face, pulled him down to her, and pressed her mouth to his.

After a moment, he began to participate, deepening the kiss. The Norseman pulled her body tightly against his and his tongue parted her lips.

The kiss was not as foreign as she had thought it would be, and the manner in which he kissed her was not what she had expected of a Norseman. His lips played upon hers like flower petals meeting in a strong breeze. Melisande surrendered to her swimming senses, to which she was becoming accustomed since she'd finished supper, and thought herself a common trollop for her actions. Nonetheless, she could find no motivation and therefore made no effort to change the wanton way in which she was behaving.

The Norseman responded by lowering them to their knees. "Melisande," he whispered against her lips.

"Melisande?" The call had come at the exact same time from somewhere in the garden.

At the sound of the intruder's voice, the Norseman's head came up. He uttered a curse and something else Melisande did not hear.

After a moment she realized who had called her and she drew in a sharp breath. "'Tis Corin!" Melisande whispered in alarm.

"Corin? Who is *Corin*?"

Her words rushed forth in panic. "Shhh... Do not speak so loudly! I pray thee, you must go."

The Norseman helped her to her feet. "This *Corin* is most likely not worthy of you."

"Melisande... Are you about?" Corin called from the opposite end of the garden.

"Corin is a gentleman and you should not judge someone whom you do not know," she scolded the nosy Norseman.

He placed his hands on her shoulders, gaining her complete attention. "Of this I do know — We shall meet again and you will not be thus attentive to this *Corin*, nor seek his attentions."

Melisande folded her arms across her chest in defiance. "Rather sure of yourself, are you not?" she demanded.

"Aye. As sure as the kiss we just shared." He took her by the hands, lifted her fingers to his lips and kissed her knuckles.

"Farewell, little star." The Norseman turned and disappeared into the shadows of the courtyard.

"Melisande…" She heard Corin call as she smoothed out the front of her gown with her hands — the hands that just moments ago had been held and tenderly kissed by the mysterious man. Melisande clutched them together as if to remember his touch. Everything still seemed to be full of cobwebs, her head, her vision…

Unsteadily, she started toward the center of the courtyard. Her stomach made a horrendous gurgle and her fists flew to her belly. Quite a ways down the yard Corin stood with his back to her. Melisande whispered a plea to her Savior that Corin did not hear her traitorous insides. She quickly tiptoed across the pliant grass and stood in front of the doorway to the ballroom, the queasiness inciting her mouth to water and a sheen of sweat causing her mask to stick to her forehead.

"Corin, why are you wandering about in the night air?" Melisande asked innocently, trying to disregard her unwell state.

"Oh, there you are, Melisande. Where have you been?" He started toward her.

Melisande's mind raced for an excuse. "Umm… Well, what are *you* doing out here?"

"I-I was looking for you."

"'Twould seem you found me." Melisande's stomach seemed to be rebelling against her and she swallowed hard. "Corin, pray excuse me. I must have a moment." She covered her mouth and ran behind a hedgerow.

"Too much wine, Melisande?" She heard him chuckle but was too engaged with being ill to address his boldness.

After part of her meal lay in the dirt in the most disgusting manner, looking half digested, she confessed from behind the bush, "Wine and rich food. Would you please fetch Lady Bergavny to me?"

"I shall be back before you notice I am gone."

"Please, feel free to take your—" She retched into the bushes again before she could finish her sentence.

When Melisande had emptied her sour stomach completely, she truly hoped Corin had heard her words, feebly delivered as they were, and would take longer than he had promised. She needed to reclaim her thoughts as well as her composure.

The Norseman seemed to be a dream, but somehow he was real. His lips had felt wonderful against hers, she thought. But then there was Corin and he was *so* handsome... She came to the conclusion that she might never see the Norseman again in any case, for she was leaving on the morrow with Helena.

"Melisande, what pains you?" Helena appeared around the hedge, Corin hovering nearby.

"My stomach, 'tis all." Embarrassed that she had consumed too much this evening, she couldn't possibly admit it, not even to Helena. "I am starting to feel better now, thank you."

Helena put her arm around Melisande's shoulder. "Let us get you inside. Mr. Sinclair, if you please, take hold of Melisande's other arm."

"Of course, my lady."

Once inside, Helena brought a small piece of bread left over from the meal to Melisande. "Eat this, and after a time that which ails you should settle."

"Thank you, Helena." Melisande took the offering but didn't dare glance at it yet. She looked at the two people gazing down at her with concern. "There will be no need for *all* of us to miss the King's masque. Please, go and enjoy yourselves."

"Melisande, I fear we have not spent enough time together on this trip. In fact, I have hardly seen you this eve," Helena offered.

"Lady Bergavny, if Melisande permits me, I shall see to her. I have attended so many of these affairs... Go and be with your lord. Melisande and I shall stay right here until the malady has passed."

Helena hesitated but only for a moment. "Gramercy, Mr. Sinclair, that is indeed gallant of you." She leaned down to give Melisande a reassuring hug and whispered, "If he tries to take advantage, call out." She straightened and looked at Corin with a placid smile. "Fitzherbert and I will be naught but three paces away if you find yourselves in need of assistance." With one more glance Melisande's way, Helena left to rejoin her husband.

Corin bowed slightly to Helena then took a seat next to Melisande. "The lady is quite motherly where you are concerned. No offense, of course."

"I can see no reason to take offense to your insightful assertion," Melisande replied and added reflectively, "Helena never had children of her own." She took a small nibble of the bread and replaced the leftover upon the table.

"You are not a child—you are very much a woman. You should have little ones of your own." After voicing his observation, he took her by the hands and gazed into her eyes with a pleasant sort of intensity. "Melisande, I realize you and I have only known each other for a day, but I so very much enjoy your company."

Melisande swallowed. "And I yours, Corin." She felt the start of flutterings in her belly that had nothing to do with her upset stomach.

"Tell me, my lady, would you ever consider an engagement to a relative of the Queen?"

"Oh, Corin, you surprise me."

"You will think on it, then?" he asked, his voice full of hope.

Melisande's smile faded. "But I leave tomorrow for Dupree, when shall I see you? I would like to get to know you at least somewhat before I consent. I have many responsibilities at home, you see."

Corin thought for a moment. "What if I came along — with an adequate escort, of course — to Dupree Castle? The time together would prove to be most beneficial for both of us."

"I should ask Helena's permission first, for I am sure she will insist that I stay one more night at Willowbrook before continuing on to Dupree."

Corin pulled her closer. "Melisande, you must come to realize that you are now at an age where you do not have to ask for things. You must *tell* her of your plans."

Melisande considered his words. "I believe you to be quite correct, Corin. I shall inform Helena before I retire this eve."

"You will not regret this, Melisande, I promise. There are some matters I must attend to before the morrow. And... I know Henry and Elizabeth will be very pleased to hear of our plans." Corin kissed both of Melisande's hands then left the room.

Melisande felt considerably better. She thought to wander over to Helena and let the good news slip out. Despite the bravery she was displaying, she still could not bring herself to *tell* Helena that she was bringing a man home with her. At least not yet.

Corin climbed into a wagon driven by one of his trusted men and minutes later they pulled out of the gates of Windsor.

At a dark crossroad just outside of London, two men on horseback waited for Corin. He didn't care that he should have been there at least four hours earlier. After all, they were hired by the Sinclairs and were paid to do what they were told.

As the conveyance pulled up, Corin moved aside the small curtain to speak to the men. "What kept you? 'Tis cold and we have ridden long and hard for a message only to return immediately —"

"Cease your prattle, or would you rather waste time chatting about court?" Corin snapped at the brigand.

"What is your word, Sinclair?" the other man demanded impatiently.

"With this final move, we'll be able to declare 'checkmate'. Dupree is all but in our hands. The lady suspects nothing. She is ignorant of our plans and is falling for me quite as I hoped she would." The end of his statement was delivered with a smug grin he couldn't stem. His brother, Jeremy, had muscle and men behind him. Corin had his looks, which had gotten him everywhere he'd wanted to be at court.

"Sounds to me that you have a soft spot for her," jeered the first man.

"Evan, the spot I have for her is far from soft. But you would not know about that sort of thing, now, would you?" Corin slashed back at him.

"Do not allow your rutting to ruin our plans, Sinclair." His voice rose, coupled with no small amount of insolence.

The second man, who was older than Evan, interrupted their banter. "Both of you, shut your mouths. I am sick of your bickering every time we encounter one another. Next time I come alone," he said pointedly to Evan.

"There will be no next time," Corin barked at the oafs. "In two days, I will be arriving at Dupree Castle. And that, my *friends*," he said sardonically, "is the message you are to take back with you. Drive on."

"Wait, Sinclair, Evan is right." The other man delayed Corin's departure. "Do not bed the wench too soon and disrupt our carefully laid plans. Timing will be essential."

"What I do with the girl is my concern, not yours nor those of our Yorkist allies. I want this to go just as smoothly as Jeremy does, if not more so. Now, tend to your business and relay my message to him," Corin said and settled back upon his seat. "Drive!" he commanded.

Once returned to the great hall, Corin mingled among the guests, for this would be his last night at court. *For now*, he mused to himself.

* * * *

A young man, masquerading as a court jester, made his way through the crowd of guests as a particularly interesting statement caught his attention.

"I plan to marry Lady Melisande Dupree before the week is out," a man dressed as a peacock bragged to another gentleman dressed as a Celt.

The jester stopped dead in his tracks, took a few inconspicuous steps toward the conversation and tilted his head to improve his chances of hearing every word.

"Have you informed your brother of this?" the Celt asked.

"I have just sent word for Jeremy and his men to meet me at Dupree for an *informal celebration* two nights hence," the peacock assured the Celt, laughing. "Indeed, it will be a celebration for the vanquisher. However, who knows how the conquered will label it?"

The Celt chuckled. "This should be an easy siege for the Sinclairs. After what happened on Frederick Chancery's grounds, you are due for a bit of good luck."

The boasting peacock gave the Celt a look of displeasure regarding his last comment and took him by the fabric of his crude costume. He spoke in hushed but gruff tones through clenched teeth. "The house of York *will* sit on the throne of England and will become more powerful than the ancient Roman Empire ever dreamed." He shoved the offending man away, stormed across the crowded room and up the winding stone stairs.

The jester pushed through the dancers, upsetting people in the way of his speedy departure. A few men shouted at him to watch his steps and everyone stopped in the middle of what they were doing, whether it was dancing or conversing, to glare at the jester, but he ignored them.

From where she stood conversing with the Bergavnys, Melisande observed a familiar-looking jester hastily cross the main floor and burst out of the doors to the garden.

After a moment more of observation, she recognized him. "Parker!" she declared under her breath. Hastily she excused herself and ran through the doors after him.

A fog was beginning to settle in the garden. Her heart thumped loudly in her ears and the damp mist felt cold and thick in her lungs. Melisande made it to the center of the courtyard just in time to see him climb the last few stairs at the top of the wall and disappear over it. Melisande followed his path and paused when she saw the end of a rope slide between two turrets on the wall. She ran to the spot, trying to see down into the inky darkness, tearing her mask and hat off to improve her vision.

The clues of this eve's riddle finally began fitting into place for Melisande — Parker... The not so unfamiliar kiss of the Norseman — "Of course! Devin!" she said in wonderment. But her heart soon sank as she remembered how she'd spoken of Corin to him. She took a deep breath and shouted over the wall into the night, "De-vin!!"

Devin shed his makeshift costume at the edge of the small copse of trees where they had hidden their horses. He was just mounting his steed when he espied Melisande high above across the lawns, looking over the wall. He made to turn and run to her when Parker, who had just come from over the wall, grabbed him fiercely by the arm. "'Twould not be wise to go to her now. We need to gather men and travel north as soon as possible."

Devin glanced at Parker but turned back to Melisande as he spoke. "Parker, it would be beneficial for you to remember your place."

"My lord, if you wish to save her we must leave at once." Parker's voice held an odd mixture of demand and beseeching.

Devin threw off Parker's hand. He wanted nothing more than to run back to Melisande's soft arms and feminine scent. He'd had just about enough of sleeping out of doors on the cold, hard ground, likely smelling of sweat and horses. His heart begged to return to the masque and his lady, when something Parker had said caught his attention.

"What do you mean, 'save her'?"

"I overheard whispers of a plot by one of the Sinclairs. They plan to take Dupree Castle by way of marriage to the Lady Melisande!"

With a curse, Devin headed for his mount. "We'll need to alert our allies, for we cannot win the day with just these few." He indicated the handful of men still with him.

"Aye. And we must hurry, for I heard they will take Dupree two days hence."

Devin swore under his breath and mounted his horse. With one final glance at Melisande, he spurred his mount forward.

Chapter Fifteen

After a somewhat lengthy amount time leaning over the wall, trying to see through the murky night air, Melisande walked as if in a trance to her room. Dismissing the Queen's attendant when she was mostly disrobed, she tossed her headdress into a corner, stripped out of her gown, and crawled into bed.

Anger and sadness seemed to be playing a game of chase with each other in her head.

How many times can I lose a man?
'You will know me by my kiss' — indeed!
I will never see him again.
He did not tell me he was the Black Knight.
I could feel him looking at me from across the room.
He again deceived me by not telling me it was he.
I long for him.
I despise him.
I love... Nay!

Melisande placed the pillows over her head in an attempt to silence the warring voices. If God was merciful this night, she'd fall asleep out of sheer exhaustion.

* * * *

"Do wake up. I need to speak with you for a moment."

Helena's voice breached the wall of peace Melisande had found that couldn't possibly have been more than an hour old. She sat up and the pillows fell from her face. "Aye?"

Helena sat on the bed next to Melisande. "I did not see you after you ran out into the gardens. I was worried—"

"Helena." Melisande took control of the conversation. "I have made a decision and wish for you and Lord Bergavny to give me your blessing."

"What is it, dear? I confess to being apprehensive about what you have to say."

"Corin Sinclair and a few of his servants will be accompanying me to Dupree. We will need to break our journey for one night at Willowbrook."

Helena lowered her gaze as if resigned to the fact that she had naught to say that would sway Melisande's decision. She finally raised her countenance to Melisande's once again, but Melisande detected a mask of granite in place of the normally friendly countenance. "Pray, lady, why would you escort Mr. Sinclair to Dupree thusly?"

Melisande suspected that Helena would not take well what she was about to say next. Resolved to stay firm in her decision, she continued, "Corin has asked for my hand and I wish to show him Dupree Castle."

Helena was silent for a few long moments. She finally sighed and nodded. "Very well, Melisande. I can see you have made up your mind," she said stiffly.

"Aye. Thank you for understanding, Helena."

"'Tis not a matter of *understanding*, 'tis merely a recognition of your words." Helena stood, opened the door and turned toward Melisande. "What of your love for Sir Devin?" she asked none too subtly.

Melisande was momentarily startled by Helena's bluntness. "I-I want a man who will tell me the truth, not one who is deceptive. I want a gentle man. Corin fits that description perfectly. He is there for me and is extremely considerate and attentive." Melisande listed her reasons as if she were trying to convince herself as well as Lady Bergavny, but pushed the thought aside.

Helena stared at her in a most knowing way. Melisande knew that once again her eyes had given her true feelings away. What could she ever hide from Helena without being found out?

"Sleep well, Melisande," Helena said flatly and shut the door.

Melisande expelled the breath she'd held. *Corin was right*, she thought. *Telling someone is much easier than groveling at their feet, asking permission.*

* * * *

The wagons were being loaded and the entourage stood nearby waiting to board when a large, cherrywood box, decorated with matching wood scrollwork fit for a king, big enough to carry at least four people inside, came forward drawn by six identical, dark brown geldings.

Corin stepped forward to inspect the thing, and Melisande and Helena exchanged glances.

"Have you ever witnessed such a sight?" Melisande whispered to Helena.

"'Tis indeed a most convenient thing to have when traveling in bad weather."

Melisande merely nodded.

Ian hailed the ladies over and Helena turned to Melisande. "My dear, would you care to sit facing forward or aft?" she asked, indicating her wagon.

Melisande glanced over at Corin. He smirked then opened the beautifully carved cherrywood door, indicating that she should join him therein.

Her gaze returned to Helena. "Corin and I will be riding in his transport," she replied matter-of-factly. Verily, she had no idea what to call it, and hadn't known previously that anything of the like even existed.

"Without a suitable companion? I hardly think—"

"I pray your pardon, Helena. *I* have made this decision as one who is in control of her own person."

She observed Helena's hands fist at her sides. "Melisande, may I have a word, *in private*?" She turned to walk in the opposite direction of the departing party.

Corin placed his hand on Melisande's arm and began to speak in a hushed tone. "Melisande, 'tis naught but folly to allow—"

"Corin, I will take her offer of conversation, but do not concern yourself. I am most confident her words will not interfere in the least with matters that are already in my itinerary." She reinforced her words by flashing him a smug grin. "Very well," Melisande called out to Helena as she gently pushed Corin's hand aside. She followed Helena around to the front of the horses.

"Aye, Helena?"

Helena expelled the breath. "It has occurred to me that this man has more influence on you than you are willing to admit."

"And just how do you mean?" Melisande enquired with a tilt of her head that she knew was less than polite.

"You have not been yourself since the masquerade last eventide and—"

"Before you waste your breath, let me explain to you that this is not Corin's doing. He merely pointed out to me that I am not a child and should not have to ask someone else's permission to live my life."

"The Queen told me that you and Corin shall be married soon. Is she correct?"

"It is as I told you, he has asked for my hand. Whether the wedding is sooner or later, it matters little." Uncomfortable with this exchange, Melisande jerked her chin to the right, unable to meet Helena's eyes. *If she prods me further I shall summon a priest to read the banns and give the mass, forthwith.*

"I do not believe you are in love with Corin, Melisande. I also do not believe he is right for you."

Melisande's gaze snapped back to Helena's. She had had enough of this discourse and raised her voice a notch or two. "Well, everyone must have thought Sir Liam was right for me—do you think *I* did?" Helena had naught to say to Melisande's revelation, so Melisande continued, "God has given me another chance at life and happiness. This decision will be mine alone to make and *no one* is going to tell me whom I shall or shall not marry." Melisande turned her back on Helena and walked around the front of the horses to Corin's side.

Corin and Melisande had started out on opposite benches but, after a short while, he moved to sit next to her, wanting to tell her a colorful jest he had once heard at a gaming table.

When he did, Melisande blushed and giggled as any delicate maiden would. "Those women do not *really* do that, do they?"

"That is what I have heard tell."

"So, you have never had one then?" He saw that she held her breath in anticipation of his answer.

Not just one. "Nay, I have not." He expertly hid his lie under a shy smile.

"That is very refreshing to hear, Corin. It merely shows that you are of noble character."

"Gramercy, my dear one…" He reached over and squeezed her hand. He knew it was time to move her with endearments and soft words. There could be no telling, once they reached Dupree, how amorous—or not—she would be toward him. At the very least, it would take a sennight for her to accept the fact that Dupree was now in the hands of the Sinclair brothers. If he moved too fast now, she may suspect… Then again, it might strike her as obligation to marry him, if only to keep the inhabitants of Dupree at ease regarding the taking of the keep and their lady. "I believe nobility of character is only recognized by another with such qualities."

Melisande smiled demurely.

The terrain became denser as they left the outskirts of London. There was a definite bite in the air and the wind howled through the trees outside. The wheels bumped and banged under them, causing the cab to rock and jump. Melisande folded her arms and shivered.

"Cold, dear one?" he asked.

"Aye." Melisande nodded.

Corin pulled the furs that covered the seat across from them over Melisande and himself. "Come closer that you may share my warmth," he offered.

She turned her back to lean against him, but Corin lifted her onto his lap instead, tucking the furs tightly around them.

Corin hid his frustration under the guise of caring suitor, gritting his teeth unnoticeably. The more he reflected upon the idea, the more he came to the conclusion that there was no reason for him to wait to bed the wench. Those men were simply jealous. Why, Jeremy would have taken her last night in the garden, ill or no. Now the game of waiting had begun — at least until they got to Dupree Castle. He cursed under his breath, disgusted that he'd allowed his brother's men to influence him in any way. The pleasure he was feeling from the weight of her body pressed intimately to his was all he could count on for now — his rampant cock wouldn't find release for some time. He glanced down at his guileless victim whose eyes were now closed peacefully. Corin's gaze raked over her lush robes. *By and by,* he told himself. *By and by.*

For a long while, Melisande had rested her head on his shoulder, every so often inhaling his fresh, clean scent. *Another advantage,* she thought. *Being a well-bred gentleman, he probably bathes more often than a knight.*

"I am not too heavy, am I?" she asked with mock coyness.

"You are perfect. I am starting to hope this bumpy journey never ends."

Melisande lifted her head just enough to see his grin and gave him one back. Then she wiggled her bum just enough to let him know she understood what he was speaking of.

"Melisande," Corin whispered hoarsely, "mind you the fire you are kindling."

She felt a great confidence stir within her and began kissing his neck. Corin seemed not to mind and tipped his head to the side in silent gesture for more. Melisande ran her lips along every inch of exposed flesh and ended by gently tugging on his earlobe with her lips. She smiled to herself and thought of Helena in the next wagon. *The lady would definitely not approve of this behavior.* She sighed and closed her eyes as she felt his hand slide inside her neckline. *Definitely not approve.* Their mutual teasing put Melisande further at ease with this gallant.

"Corin," she whispered against his ear. "'Tis quite warm now."

Corin peeled away the furs and tossed them to the floor. He then reclined onto the bench, taking Melisande with him. With his hands he pushed upward just underneath her breasts so that the white mounds of her bosom peeked over her neckline. As Corin trailed kisses over her décolletage then up her throat, she surrendered fully to her passions. Recalling how Devin's hands had felt on her body, she longed for Corin to make her feel that way now. "Corin," she whispered. "I want you to take me."

Corin groaned into the skin at her neck. "Oh, Melisande. I want you, so very much…" He sat up slightly so that he could look into her eyes. "But I want it to be perfect for you, not in some cramped wooden box. I want it to be in a large, soft bed, with a fire roaring in the hearth, and wine… It is how I want our wedding night to be."

Melisande buried her face into his velvet tabard.

"Please do not feel that I am rejecting you. I believe you deserve much more than this cab and bench."

After a few silent moments had passed, Corin addressed her. "Are you upset with me, love?"

Melisande shook her head. "Nay, merely out of breath, 'tis all," she murmured. Several more moments went by before she looked up at him. "I must admit, Corin, I do admire you for your restraint." She blushed, embarrassed by her own wanton aspirations, and placed her head back upon his chest. As Melisande drifted off to sleep, she weighed the vast differences between Corin and Devin.

* * * *

Melisande awoke to Corin stroking her cheek with his thumb. "We have arrived at Willowbrook, dear one. You just missed Lady Helena. She opened the door to our conveyance unannounced, poked her head in and let me know that her valet would show me to my rooms in the west tower."

"Was she very upset?"

"Well, she shut the door as abruptly as she had opened it, if that is any indication."

"Most likely she was not pleased by our closeness."

"I would say she was just slightly vexed." Corin's lips curved into a smile.

"An extreme understatement, I am most certain," Melisande purred. She sat up and moved the small curtain aside.

Corin took her hand and drew her from the window. "Do not worry, love, it will not be long until we are wed and no one will have cause to judge our actions."

Melisande gave his hand a thankful squeeze and started out of the door.

Instantly, Maggie and Tilly came rushing forward.

"M'lady, how did you fare?" Maggie asked. "And from where did this immodest conveyance come? Why, it's the size of Noah's Ark."

"Good heavens, is this how people are getting from place to place these days?" Tilly enquired with wonder in her voice. "It seems London is indeed as fanciful as they say!"

"Is it true that you played for King Henry?" Maggie cooed, practically swooning.

Both of the girls fell silent and stared over their mistress's head. Melisande whirled around, expecting to see a two-headed dragon swooping down from the sky, but it was only Corin emerging from the conveyance.

Melisande turned back to her maids. "Close your mouths, girls, or you are liable to swallow a fly." She strode forward, mounted the stairs that led into Willowbrook's great hall and waited for Corin at the top.

Corin nodded a polite bow to each of them and they stumbled over each other to curtsy back. He stepped past them, winked at Melisande as he passed, then followed the Willowbrook valet up the stairs in the direction of the west tower.

The two maids stood there staring after him, their eyes wide.

"Did you see him, Maggie?" Tilly asked as if in a trance.

"We must get to London," Maggie said flatly.

"Aye. Soon," Tilly agreed.

Melisande quelled a grin. She would have protested had their banter not been entirely accurate about the vision that was Corin.

Once Corin was out of sight, Melisande searched even into the deep corners of every room for Devin, but he was nowhere to be found. At one point, she ran up the stairs to her chamber and flung open her door, expecting him to be waiting inside. He was not. She walked speedily and light-footed to his door and hesitated as she placed her hand on the rough oak. She gave a push and took a step in. His scent permeated her very existence and the bittersweet memories of that night, the sensations she could almost feel, flooded her mind. But no Devin. Melisande stepped back and shut the heavy door.

Just then a maid rounded the corner. "M'lady, Sir Devin is not at Willowbrook. We have not seen him for nearly half a sennight now."

Melisande was sick of maids who gossiped and revealed eagerly what was none of their business. "I must have the wrong room," Melisande remarked, and hurried back to her chamber.

Melisande had thrown herself onto her bed for a good crying fit when Maggie and Tilly flew into the chamber.

"M'lady, where did you find *him*?" Tilly asked, incredulously.

"Who is he?" Maggie echoed with the same enthusiasm.

"He is simply magnificent," Tilly exclaimed.

"Are all the men in London *that* handsome?" Maggie asked in wonderment.

Tilly's and Maggie's questions tumbled out of their mouths one after the other, each girl barely giving the other time enough to finish her enquiry.

Melisande swallowed her emotions, unwilling to divulge her thoughts and appear even more fickle than she felt. "I met him at Windsor, he is a relative of the Queen, his name is Corin Sinclair, and nay, not all of the men in London are *that* handsome."

"A relative of the Queen!" Maggie squealed.

"How divine!" Tilly said, clasping her hands together and tilting her face toward heaven.

"Did you see his eyes!" Maggie declared to the room in general.

They stopped their bantering long enough to ask the next question in unison.

"What is he about *here*?"

Melisande exhaled an exasperated sigh, preparing herself for the explosion that her forthcoming answer would surely initiate. "Corin has petitioned me for my hand."

Both girls made a long, ear-piercing squeak.

"There should be a celebration!" Tilly declared.

"Halt." Melisande's hand came up in front of the two girls as she loudly pronounced, "I have had enough celebrating to last me quite some time, thank you." Melisande's tone softened somewhat. "Please go, I would like to rest before supper."

Maggie and Tilly chattered all the way down the corridor and Melisande rolled her gaze heavenward in an appeal to God.

As she sat on her bed, she decided against crying over Devin. Corin was considerate, strong and visually stunning, his bloodline connected him to the throne — he was almost too perfect to be real. What more did she need? Melisande stripped out of her surcoat and, atop her bed, drifted to sleep.

* * * *

It was not long before Melisande's maids came in with steaming buckets of water, followed by four men carrying a waist-high wooden tub that they placed near the hearth.

It was most hospitable of Helena to have ordered the bath, regardless of their disagreement earlier.

On their way out one of the men patted Tilly on her bum whilst she lined the tub with fabric. Melisande caught the action and shooed Maggie after she'd poured the water, telling her that she would take care of her bath and dress herself, then she dismissed them both.

It was not too difficult to remove the rest of her clothing. A few seams ripped open, and lacings were pulled from the garment when they would not come undone, but she could not stand to be in the same room with her promiscuous maids. The second after that thought had passed so clearly through her mind, another one came in just as loud and resounding as that one had been. *Judge not, that ye be not judged. For with what judgment ye judge, ye shall be judged, and with what measure ye mete, it shall be measured to you again.* Melisande understood well the word that had been given to her.

Donning a white linen bathing gown, she stepped into the tub and began to wash. As the warm water seeped into the bones of her legs and feet, she realized that her actions of the past few days were no different from those of her maids. Devin had not proposed marriage and she really didn't know Corin at all.

It did not take long for the water to go cold, for the weather had turned from a sunny day with a strong north wind to a dark, ominous one. The stone walls of Willowbrook seemed to soak up what was being provided for them outside. It would only take a day or two for the storm to hit full force. Storms were so easy to predict, for she had seen many of the like. Pity she couldn't read men in such a way.

Melisande wrapped a large length of cloth around her body and sat before the hearth on a pile of furs to comb out her wet hair. When it was dry, and she had finished with the braid she had coiled at the nape of her neck, the memory of what Corin had said to her the night of the masquerade came back to her. *'After you have your bath, I will brush out your hair until it is dry…'* The rest of what he had said was not very clear.

I remember now. The King's wine. She grimaced. *How could something taste so good yet have such adverse effects?* With the exception of the wine, would being married to Corin be like that every night? He was so very handsome. He made her feel wanted, something she thought she'd never feel again owing to how Devin had misused her heart.

Tears formed, blurring her vision. *No.* She stood and went to the edge of the bed where her night-rail lay waiting for her. Dropping the drying fabric behind her, she pulled the gown over her head. She would deny herself the luxury of crying, for what good did it do? Besides, she was likely overtired and needed a rest before supper.

Peeling back the coverlet, she sank onto the mattress and burrowed beneath the pillows.

Chapter Sixteen

At supper, Melisande kept her thoughts of Devin averted by watching Corin and studying his mannerisms. He was truly a beautiful man and the courtly etiquette he displayed was impeccable. Once he even winked at her over his wine, which Melisande thought rather mischievous of him.

"Melisande?" Until now, Helena hadn't spoken to her since they'd arrived. "I would like to see you after supper, if it is your wish also, of course."

Melisande felt a twinge of guilt. "Of course. I am finished now."

"Shall we, then?"

As she and Helena departed from the room, Lord Bergavny invited Corin to a game of chess.

Helena waved over two servants who then cloaked them in fur-lined, hooded garments.

"I wanted to speak with you in privacy" — she indicated the door — "where we won't be disturbed."

Melisande decided not to be contradictory this time. Moments later, she and Helena started out for the gardens in silence, clutching the cloaks tightly about their necks. Melisande stared at the high-backed bench atop which she and Devin had shared their first kiss. As they passed it, Helena spoke. "This morning when I told you that you were acting differently, I was wrong. 'Tis I who am being childish."

"I—" Melisande clamped her jaw shut and attempted to keep her assessments of the situation to herself. Recovering, she continued with as much grace as she could muster. "How do you mean?"

"When you first came into my care for the games, I felt as if I had a daughter of my own."

"My dear Helena, I never meant to—"

Helena turned to her, halting their progress upon the path. Out from under her cloak, she gently raised a hand to stop Melisande's refute. "Please, let me finish." Melisande nodded her acquiescence. "It was not proper of me to take over the role of your mother. You have been on your own for quite a while now and were correct when you spoke your mind to me on the matter. I am truly sorry. Do forgive me."

How could Melisande refuse such an elegant apology? Melisande reached out, clasped Helena's free hand in her own, and looked her in the eye. "Now 'tis my turn to apologize. The things I said to you today and the way in which I said them were not how one adult treats another and I am heartily sorry for it."

"Thank you. However, your feelings of regret are not necessary. You were only reacting to a situation in the heat of the moment. But if it is any consolation, you are also forgiven."

With a much lighter heart, now that the rift between them had been repaired, Melisande and Helena made their way back to the warm hall where the men were laughing at the game they'd just finished.

"That, son, was the fastest game I have ever played." Lord Bergavny chuckled.

"I have never really been taught to play properly." Corin's face had gone red and Melisande found it endearing.

After placing their cloaks into the waiting hands of a servant, Melisande came to rest upon one of the intricately carved wooden benches that sat before a great cast-iron ingle while Helena exchanged a few words with Lord Bergavny.

As Corin made himself comfortable next to Melisande, she whispered to him, "You lost on purpose, did you not?"

Corin grinned. "'Tis Fitzherbert's home — just *how* did you know of my honorable deception?" he enquired quietly, his eyes alight with mirth.

She smiled and said close to his ear, "I know that you are a discerning gentleman in more ways than one."

Corin tilted his head toward her. "You know me so well, do you?" he asked and put his arm behind Melisande's back. She shrugged and snuggled in close, tucking her feet under her skirts on the bench next to her.

Thunder rumbled in the distance.

"'Tis quite a storm we are about to encounter," Melisande commented.

"Aye, I have not seen a storm such as this in a good many years," Lord Bergavny replied, as he and Helena took seats across from them.

"I hope it will not last so long as to hinder our travel plans for the morrow," Corin stated, mostly to himself.

"Indeed," Melisande agreed.

Lady Bergavny mumbled something Corin didn't quite hear and Lord Bergavny cleared his throat.

"Melisande, would you be so kind as to play for us, if only to keep our minds off the storm?"

"A splendid idea. I would love to play for you."

Melisande had hopped up to fetch an instrument when Helena spoke. "Let one of your maids retrieve your—"

"Nay. I wish to choose one."

Corin looked on as she dashed up the stairs and turned down the left corridor.

Once Melisande was out of hearing range, the Lady of Willowbrook seized the opportunity to enquire of Corin's plans for the future. "When do you and Melisande plan to marry, Mr. Sinclair?"

"Actually, I am waiting for Melisande to accept my proposal. When she does agree to be my wife, we shall wed immediately, I assure you," he said quite confidently. "A relative of the royal court need not wait for the banns to be read."

"Mmm." Helena didn't reply any more than that, which suited Corin just fine.

Melisande came back with her lute and sat down on a stool.

Melisande played beautifully for quite some time and a barrage of servants came into the hall to light several more candles and feed the ingle's dwindling embers with peat and wood. Corin couldn't wait to play the master of Dupree and order the serfs there to see to his various comforts beneath his own roof.

As Melisande laid her instrument down, Corin stood up and strode over to her. "I shall never tire of hearing you perform. Will you play for me privately, once we are wed, love?"

Melisande stood. "Any time you desire it." She smiled.

Corin paused and traced a line over her cheek. "Does this mean you have come to a decision regarding our betrothal?"

Melisande nodded, and he embraced the girl hard as if it would assist in solidifying her answer.

At once, Lady Bergavny excused herself, half dragging her lord from the room.

Ignoring the hasty departure of the Bergavnys, Corin kissed Melisande. *Marriage to this beauty certainly won't be a chore*, he predicted. After a few moments, he felt moisture touch his cheek. He pulled away to look into her eyes. "What is it, dear one?"

"I am sorry, Corin. I really do not know. Mayhaps it is the impulsiveness of it all. For years, I thought I'd never give myself away in marriage again."

Corin led her back to the bench. "Let us sit quietly for a while," he said softly and put his arms around her as a comfort. *I have come this far with this girl and will not lose her to any childish fears*, he mused, then wondered how the siege was progressing. He had not allowed himself to think about it for over twelve hours now, for fear that it would show in his face. *Mayhaps bedding the wench now will erase the smallest trace of apprehension she might possess.*

By the warm glow of the fire Melisande had fallen asleep wrapped in his arms and he dozed off and on, hardly able to quiet his mind over the coming tempests—the weather outside and the capture of Dupree.

A servant girl stepped into the room. "Beggin' yer pardon, sir, mum?"

"What is it?" Corin whispered so as not to wake Melisande.

"M'lord and lady have retired for the evenin' and I am to see to yer's and Lady Dupree's needs."

"Very well, we shall inform you if we are in need."

The moment the servant had quit the room, Melisande's eyelids fluttered open and she stared at the low fire.

"Hungry?"

"Not particularly at the moment. You?"

"Not too. I am enjoying this—you sleeping in my arms... The fire..."

"If the rest of our life is like this, Corin, I shall be the happiest woman in England."

He smiled and kissed her on the top of her head. *If you promise to obey I shall be the happiest of men.* "Here, let me take down your hair. Having it pulled back like that must get uncomfortable at times."

Melisande sat up and presented her back to him.

Corin gently tugged at the ribbon and untwined the three thick strands. He ran his fingers through the light-golden waves and inhaled her scent.

Aye. Quite the prize.

Melisande exhaled a soft sigh of pleasure. "You are correct. It feels wonderful to have it down."

"I should like you to wear it this way as we travel." He rubbed the silky locks possessively between his fingertips.

"I will have to fight my maids, but I shall win the day for you." She giggled.

"Your maids?"

"Aye, they insist I have a hat on, or at the very least braids coiled on top of my head. Verily, 'tis but trivial stuff and utter nonsense." They laughed together and Melisande settled back into his arms.

He listened to and interpreted her sigh. Within the sound he detected more discontent than wistfulness.

"What thoughts plague you this eve, my dear?" he asked her, feeling slightly anxious that she might unkiss their agreement.

"Nay. Nothing to concern yourself with," she replied.

The wood on the fire crackled. For a moment, he allowed himself to imagine that he could have something like this with her. However, once he tried to visualize her conforming to his plans as the conquered should when their castle was taken, he suspected that such an ideal situation might never come to pass.

"Corin?"

"Aye?

She turned in his arms to look at him. "You are everything a woman could want, and I fear I do not deserve you."

Corin chuckled. "Then you must gain a higher opinion of yourself."

"I?"

"Mm. Imagine if you will, for a moment, living in the King's palace."

"Oh, I could never…" she replied, looking away.

"And why not?"

"Well, it is so…so…*extravagant*."

"Melisande. When we are married, I plan to lavish you with extravagance." Her look of surprise was quite charming. "Did you think everything would stay the same once we become husband and wife?"

"In honesty, I never thought about it."

"Do not worry your pretty little head over this. I will take care of everything."

She smiled and reclined against him once again.

By and by, Melisande sat up. "I think I might like to have a little something to eat now."

"Very well. You rest here and I shall fetch us a bite or two from the larder." He arose from the bench and placed a brief kiss on her forehead.

"You are a very thoughtful man." She smiled up at him.

"I am at your beck and call, dear one."

Once Corin had left the room, Melisande jumped up, grabbed her lute then hurried up the stairs.

"Good eventide, m'lady." Maggie stood, ceasing her packing for the trip back to Dupree. "Your hair! It—"

"Never mind the state of my hair, Maggie, where are my sleeping gown and winter robe?" Melisande asked in haste, placing her lute at the foot of the bed.

"I shall fetch them out of the trunk for you." Maggie rushed over to one of the trunks and dug around until she found the garments.

"Where is Tilly?" Melisande asked as Maggie helped her off with her tunic.

"Saying farewell to..." She finished slowly, as if reluctant to share the information. "Some friends of ours from Willowbrook."

"Friends, hmm?" she replied, unable to hide her smirk.

"Aye, m'lady. We did, after all, have some time on our hands while you were in London, and—"

"I hope in nine months' time, your bellies are not so swollen that you cannot help me dress," Melisande half teased

"Oh, nay, m'lady, never."

At the concern on Maggie's countenance, Melisande spun away from her maid with her hand on her own abdomen, belatedly hoping that Devin's seed had not taken root within her.

"M'lady, are you ready to be dressed?"

"Indeed, of course." Melisande turned back to Maggie for assistance with the chemise.

The very second Maggie was finished, Melisande burst forth from her chamber. She paused at the top of the stairs to catch her breath and smooth her hair over one shoulder.

Just as she returned to the bench in front of the fire, Corin appeared carrying a large assortment of food.

"So, is that where you had run off to? I came back to ask if you wanted your cider warmed and you were gone."

"I wanted to be more comfortable. Do you find it agreeable?" She stood and twirled around for him.

Corin set the salver upon a table and approached Melisande, his beautiful dark brown gaze penetrating into her very soul. "It matters naught what you wear, dear one. In fact, you must look even better without anything at all covering your skin," he said as he lifted a curl from her breast.

"You rogue," she said, and playfully hit him with the sleeve of her robe. Corin pulled her to him and kissed her ravenously. She complied, losing herself in the action.

"Corin, I am hungry," she said against his lips.

"As I am, my lady," he growled.

"I think we should eat now, I mean."

Corin chuckled. He brought the food to Melisande and they sat.

They played through the late snack, laughing, teasing and feeding each other little bites of bread and meat. He showed her how sucking on each other's fingertips and kissing away bits of food from lips and chins could be oh so arousing. As her belly filled, her appetite for fulfillment increased. *After all, he's been most considerate this night and has treated me with a wondrous mix of respect and care for my person...* Melisande pushed aside the fact that she was trying desperately to convince herself that this was the correct course.

Redirecting her attention to the situation at hand, she observed Corin in the red-orange glow of the firelight. His every move and deed focused on her, his attentiveness drawing her heart closer and closer to him.

Corin set aside the salver and took her in his arms. "You have both a question and its answer in your eyes, dear one."

Aye, she wanted him to make love to her. Why should she now deny herself the pleasure?

Without another word, he scooped up Melisande as if she weighed less than a single stone and headed up the stairs toward her chamber. When they came to the door, they heard the maids talking and carrying on inside.

"What about your room?"

"No privacy there. One of my men—that is, my valet—sleeps on a cot at the end of the bed."

"This must not have been meant to be," she whispered, her disappointment audible.

He nuzzled her neck. "How big is your bed at Dupree?"

"We could lose each other in it."

"I cannot wait." He put her down and kissed her tenderly. "Until the morrow, I shall think of you every moment."

Melisande grinned as she shooed him down the hall. Once through her door, she tiptoed across the floor. Avoiding her busy maids, she crawled into bed, thrilled to be so desired by Corin Sinclair, her future husband.

Chapter Seventeen

It was before dawn when Melisande was dragged out of bed. However, one would have thought that it was the middle of the night. The sky was filled with the black clouds that had been gathering since the day before, and a chilling wind was just beginning to stir. She needed to be properly dressed for the day's journey, her maids insisted. The traveling costume consisted of a long-sleeved tunic in pale peach and a dark brown surcoat that reached to the ground in a straight skirt. Low riding boots covered her feet to mid-calf, and she wore thick wool hose that reached to her upper legs for warmth. A soft brown leather belt was fastened high above her waist, and after a long, drawn-out battle over Melisande's hair, Tilly had brushed it out so that it fell in golden curls over her shoulders and down her back. The outfit was finished off with a brown, squirrel fur-lined wrap.

The wagons were being loaded out front as Helena and Melisande said their final farewells near the entrance to the great hall.

"Do have care on your journey and keep warm," Helena advised as she pulled Melisande's wrap tighter around her shoulders.

"I shall, and I will send word of the wedding feast. You and Lord Bergavny will attend, will you not?"

"We shall await your word." Helena took Melisande by the hands, looked straight into her eyes, and spoke softly. "Before you take the final step, listen to your heart." Helena's tears spilled down her cheeks then.

"May God grant thee mercy, Helena," Melisande said as she tightly hugged her friend and swallowed the lump of emotion that had formed in her throat.

"And you," Helena whispered.

Corin came down the stairs to the main hall with his servants in tow. "Shall we be off, my lady?" He smiled as he offered Melisande his forearm.

She smiled back at him when she accepted his escort and placed her hand onto his wrist. At once she thought about how lovely her life would be from this moment on.

Out of doors, Lord Bergavny had been seeing to the final preparations for Melisande and Corin's journey, and he greeted them when they emerged from the great hall of Willowbrook.

"Well, my dear, everything awaits your pleasure. I pray you have a swift and unencumbered journey home."

"I thank you, Lord Bergavny, you have been a most courteous host."

"And I thank you for gracing us with your talents."

Melisande curtsied and he placed a kiss on both her cheeks. Lord Bergavny clasped hands with Corin and he and Melisande stepped down to the caravan.

Tilly and Maggie came around to the front of one of the wagons. "Which will you be riding in, m'lady?"

Tilly enquired of her mistress, her eyes respectfully downward.

"I shall ride in Mr. Sinclair's and you and Maggie shall be riding in mine."

Maggie's protest came from behind Tilly as both their gazes snapped to Melisande. "But, m'lady, surely —"

Melisande raised her hand to cut off Maggie's words. "That will be my final word on the subject," she said firmly. Melisande wondered how she'd ever gotten along without her newfound authority.

She watched as her maids glanced up at Helena with worried looks about their faces. Helena pleasantly smiled at them through her tears and nodded once in support of Melisande. Reluctantly, they climbed into the Dupree wagon, then Corin helped Melisande into his.

The whips snapped at the front and Melisande watched through the small window as they passed Helena and Lord Bergavny. Helena waved with one hand and mopped at her tears with the other. Lord Bergavny placed his arm around his wife's shoulders. "Godspeed," he called out.

Melisande had many times tried to start a conversation with Corin, but ever since they'd departed from Willowbrook he'd seemed distant. Giving up, she sat quietly in the corner and eventually the motion rocked her to sleep.

A loud clap of thunder startled Melisande awake and she looked out of the small portal. The rain came down in heavy sheets. She glanced over at her traveling companion and saw that his countenance seemed stormy as well. "Corin, is aught amiss? Will all be well for our journey home?"

"If everything goes as expected," he replied shortly, as if she had asked the question many times over the course of the trip.

It was more words than he had said all morning, yet it was a strange answer to her enquiry. She pondered it a moment longer then asked, "Are you hungry?"

"I ate while you were sleeping." He retrieved a bundle from a basket on the floor and set it next to her. He sounded cordial enough—however, there wasn't even a hint of a smile on his face.

"Why did you not awaken me?"

He shrugged. "I did not wish to disturb your slumber. You seemed quite at peace."

Melisande decided to voice the slight frustration she had with him. "You seem out of sorts or...overly concerned about something, Corin. Is it the storm?"

"Aye, the storm." He finally gave her a smile. However, there was no evidence of it in his eyes.

She dismissed the change in his personality and opened the bundle of bread and cheese. "Have no fear, Corin. I have yet to see lightning strike a conveyance in motion," she teased just before she took a bite of the fare. When she'd finished, she retied the bundle and placed it on the seat opposite her and Corin. "I left some bread if you are hungry later."

"Thank you," he said flatly, not turning from gazing out of the small window on his side.

Melisande stretched and yawned loudly. Although an unladylike action, she felt comfortable in their nest of privacy.

"Are you still tired, dear one?" he asked, looking at her for the first time in what seemed hours.

"Pray forgive me, my maids were quite loud as they arranged and rearranged my trunks almost until we left this morn."

"Come. Place your head on my legs and stretch out as much as possible on the rest of the bench," he insisted.

As she did, Corin covered her with furs and drew the fabric across the portal to block out the light. Within no time her thoughts drifted into slumber again.

* * * *

A particularly large rut in the road caused Melisande to awaken and she hastily sat up on the bench. Moving the thick fabric aside, she peeked out of the window. Finally, the last stretch of road was upon them. It had rained inconsistently all day, yet slow was the going. The mud from the wet roads likely hindered the wheels, making it difficult for the horses to get through. She could see that they were just approaching the outskirts of Dupree property. "It will not be long now," Melisande said confidently.

Corin's tense impatience showed from his face and shoulders down his arms to his clenched fists. "Unless the road is completely washed away," Corin spat through his teeth.

Melisande watched Corin as he looked out of the opposite window and ran the snarls out of her hair with her fingers. When she was satisfied with her self-appointed task, she turned toward her window. "It seems to get slower as we come closer."

Corin whipped his head around to glare at her. "Aye, and you speaking of it is not helping the situation," he snapped.

She turned to him and their gazes locked. Melisande could not decide if she should be angry with the way he was treating her or hurt by it when she noticed the tiny beads of sweat on his upper lip.

"Tell me, Corin, are you still vexed about the storm?"

He did not answer. He merely turned back to his window.

Melisande folded her arms across her chest, jerking her chin in the opposite direction. *He is as nervous as a field mouse.*

It wasn't long after that they pulled through the castle gates. Melisande thought it odd that there were no sentries posted upon the parapets as there usually were. The sun had recently set and the storm clouds provided an eerie glow but that certainly wasn't reason for the lack of guards.

The rain poured down torrentially now as the driver of Corin's conveyance pulled to a stop very close to the stone steps.

"I cannot imagine what my servants are about," she commented as she looked to every corner for someone.

Corin quickly helped Melisande on with her cloak. "I am sure they are engaged elsewhere." He turned from her, shoved open the door, exited the conveyance and took the steps two at a time.

Melisande thought it was strange that he did not wait for her — after all it was *her* home. She figured it must have been the rain that drove him inside so quickly. Melisande entered the great hall not moments after Corin and shook out her skirts. Again, not a single soul from Dupree greeted them.

It was Corin himself who shut the door and slid the heavy, iron-bound wooden bolt home.

"Corin, my maids will be unloading my instruments through that door," she stated as she slid her cloak from her shoulders and placed it upon a bench just inside the doorway.

"Nay, they will not," he replied as if the conversation was over.

"Corin, what has gotten into—" Melisande stopped, having noticed the crowd of strange men looking at her and Corin. They sat scattered about the hall like so much litter. A bad feeling began in her belly and spread to her limbs. "Pray, who are you and where are my servants?"

The men blatantly laughed at her.

"Hail, Sinclair!" A jovial voice came from the crowd. One of the men stood up and started walking toward Melisande and Corin.

Melisande backed up against Corin for safety. "What is this?" she asked just above a whisper.

"We are your new staff," the tall, broad, rough-looking man jested with a sweep of his hand. The room lit up with laughter.

Somewhere in the back of Melisande's mind she detected a hint of a Highlander's accent among the murmurings of the scoundrels who had somehow obtained entrance to her home.

Corin held out his hand and grasped the other man's arm in friendship. "It has been a long time, Erik."

"Too long, Corin. You are still as ugly as sin, though!" The men who were gathered around the tables and brazier, shared laughter between them, as if a private jest had been presented.

"Where is Jeremy?" Corin asked the man.

Erik raked Melisande from head to toe with an insolent gaze, then focused back on Corin and winked. "Jeremy is otherwise occupied."

The assembled men in the room hooted and whistled.

Melisande stepped away from Corin and whirled around. "Explain this invasion of my home, Corin Sinclair," she demanded, growing more furious by the moment. "Who do you think you are, inviting these— these *people* into my home?"

"Erik, would you please excuse Lady Dupree and me? I believe the time has come to let her in on our little secret."

The man Erik leered at Melisande once again. He elbowed Corin in the ribs and spoke as if she were not even in the room. "I'll wager she's a tasty morsel of flesh." He swaggered back to the men and said something to them that Melisande did not hear. They grunted, whistled and made lewd noises at Corin and Melisande.

Corin led Melisande to the top of the stairs and into the first chamber he could find. "Very nice, Melisande. It has a feminine touch and yet seems strong," he remarked, mocking her, she was sure.

"Corin, if you wanted your own staff to move in, why did you not just ask? And how could you tolerate such impertinence from them?"

"Love, I am afraid you do not understand. The Sinclairs have *taken* Dupree Castle in the name of the house of York and Elizabeth Stuart."

"No. I don't believe it. Who is York?"

"That is right, you are still young and would not remember the War of the Roses."

"I do. I remember that it is over. Corin, you had best be forthcoming, for my patience is already in shreds."

Corin gave Melisande a smug grin. "Queen Elizabeth Stuart is of the House of York," he explained.

"Nay, Queen Elizabeth is married to our king, Henry Tudor, and is now such."

"Well, that is also correct, but there are those of us who think Elizabeth of York should have the throne for herself. *She* should be the rightful ruler over England."

"She would never go against the King. 'Twould be treason!"

"Regardless, we intend to take the throne and give the crown to Queen Elizabeth Stuart."

"Correct me if I am wrong, but the Queen has no knowledge of this, does she?"

Corin grinned at Melisande, and she wondered how she had ever seen him as handsome.

"We were hoping it would be a surprise," he drawled lazily.

"'Twill never happen!" she yelled. "You and your horde of bandits will be executed before Elizabeth ever hears of this scandal!"

"And just who will foil our plans, *you*?"

"Mayhaps."

Corin grabbed Melisande roughly by the arms. "I will give you one chance to join this fight and stand by my side as my wife or be trampled with the rest of Henry's loyal subjects. You may choose the easy path or the difficult one. Which will it be?"

"I will never join with you — in marriage *or* war." She held fast to her courage and spat in Corin's face.

Corin shoved her across the room and she fell, tripping on her long surcoat.

Wiping his face on his sleeve, he glared down at her.

She attempted to rise, but her boots were all tangled within the fabric of her gown.

He bounded after her and dropped to the floor, only to hold her down with his body. She could feel his hot breath on her face and it nearly made her retch.

"You have made your choice, but mark my words. I will have what is coming to me, you little tease. Erik!" he bellowed down to the men. "Have someone open the tower for the *former* mistress of Dupree."

Two men appeared at the top of the stairs and Corin pushed himself up from atop Melisande. She kicked her skirts aside, gathered herself up off the floor and tried to run past the men. Without much effort on their parts, they caught her by the arms and took her down a corridor and up two more long stretches of stairs toward the tower.

Inside the tower room was as cold and dank as any pit in Christendom must have been. A third man appeared with a torch to light the others around the circular room. All three men departed and she heard a heavy piece of wood fall across the outside of the door, likely blocking any attempt at escape.

Melisande pounded on the door until her fists felt bruised. She paced around the room, too angry to cry and too infuriated to think clearly. After some time had passed, she collapsed in the center of the room and her tears came with the help of gut-wrenching sobs, strong enough to strip her throat of skin, making her sick to her stomach.

Dear God. Helena was right.

Chapter Eighteen

The door flew open and Melisande rolled over on the cold stone floor, shivering, oblivious to whether it was day or night. The torches had long since burned out and her eyes stung from crying.

"There now, let me warm you."

"Corin?" Melisande asked as she felt a pile of furs tossed across her feet. "Corin, why are you allowing this happen to me? To my home?"

"Shhh... Do not speak," the husky male voice urged as Melisande was pulled to a seated position.

Two arms wrapped around Melisande. Her body said stay, but her heart and mind simultaneously screamed a warning. She started to weep and tried to shrug away from the human touch. The arms tightened around her roughly and she was pulled again to the ground. A demanding hand slid up her leg and came to rest atop her naked thigh, squeezing, kneading.

"Nay!" she screamed as she clenched her knees together, blocking the probing fingers from venturing further.

"Just a quick fuck... I have in my possession where you dwell and now I must also have you," the voice whispered gruffly against her ear and a not so freshly shaven jaw scraped against her cheek. As he kissed her, he left cold wet spots where his lips touched her neck and face.

Melisande tried futilely to twist her body away from the vile assailant. She could only guess that the man she had almost taken to her bed at Willowbrook was now in her company. In one quick motion, her leg came up and connected with his groin, and he rolled away from her, moaning in pain. It was most unfortunate that he now blocked her only retreat.

With renewed vigor, Melisande leaped to her feet and backed up against the wall.

The shadowed figure staggered to an upright position. It only took him two strides to reach her. "You bloody bitch!" he shrieked and he slammed the back of his hand into her cheek.

She found herself on the ground again, this time holding the side of her face with her hand, attempting in vain to see through the evanescence of stars before her eyes.

"I will never, ever warm your bed, Corin Sinclair!" she yelled through her pain in his general direction.

He laughed. "I am sorry, Lady Dupree, we have not been properly introduced." He paused and she heard him walk across the floor of her prison. "I am Jeremy Sinclair, Corin's twin brother." And with that, he took his exit and threw the door shut, and she heard the wooden barrier as it was slammed back into its holder.

Still in pain from the assault, Melisande crawled over to the furs, covered her body, and cried herself into exhaustion.

* * * *

The rain continued through the wee hours of the morning. Melisande awoke to the musty smell of her cell mixed with the ominous feeling of certain doom. She decided to sit against the oak door so that she could be alerted sooner if someone approached. She gathered the furs, her only saving grace from the night before, and laid her head against the old wood. She had lived in this castle for almost five years and only once walked past the stairs that led to the room, not paying any mind either to the stairs nor the room.

As she looked about, she noticed one shutter-covered window, which she had not noticed in the dark when she was brought in last eve. High upon the wall it was, yet just low enough to be accessible. If she rolled the furs into a tight ball and stood on them, and if she stretched up onto the tips of her toes, she could reach it. Then, if God would be merciful, she might be able to pull herself up and escape through it.

She went to the window and divested herself of her surcoat to add to the makeshift step. She stood on top of the pile and pulled at the shutter. It felt as if it were a part of the stone wall. She pried at the wood with all her might and it finally swung open with such force that it crashed inward, still attached to the wall by its crude rope hinges. At the sound of footsteps, Melisande ran back to the door, put her ear to it, and listened for a moment. It must have been her imagination, for not a sound could be heard in the corridor. She went back to the window, pulled herself up, and climbed through the portal. Once she was out of the tower, she lowered herself over the side of the wall walk. For a moment, she dangled by her hands, fearful of the long drop to the battlements below.

* * * *

"So, you have not bedded the wench as of yet, brother?" Jeremy Sinclair taunted his twin.

"Nay, but don't think that I couldn't. After all, 'twas she who confessed to the wanting of me, even before I suggested it," Corin casually stated with an aristocratic wave of his hand.

Jeremy laughed with a mouth full of meat and the sound echoed through the hall. "I just might have to ask her if that is true or not," he replied, as if he didn't believe him.

"Why do you not ask her now, Jeremy?" Erik said as he pushed Melisande into the room, both of them soaked to the skin. "I found her running across the courtyard toward the gatehouse."

Jeremy stood and strode over to her. "I am impressed," he sneered, circling her like a cat about to pounce on a mouse. "I would never have guessed you had it in you to attempt such a feat." Then Jeremy snapped at Erik. "Show me exactly how she escaped and we'll make sure it doesn't happen again." He and Erik crossed the room to the doors. "She is a feisty one. You always knew how to pick the women, brother," Jeremy commented wryly over his shoulder, and they quit the hall.

Helpless and alone, Melisande lifted her gaze to glare at Corin. He stood and walked toward her. She made to recoil when he grabbed her arm, but he caught her regardless. "Back to the tower — I mean, your chamber, m'lady."

He pushed her up the main stairs and down the corridor to the longer staircases that led to the tower.

Clutching her upper arm with a vise-like grip, Corin lifted the heavy plank with one hand and tossed it aside. Once inside, he threw her in and shut the door behind them.

Melisande couldn't believe her escape attempt had been thwarted. She hadn't been three steps from the gates when that Erik had snatched her up and dragged her back into the hall to her captors.

"Now I am going to do my part to make sure you do not try to escape again." He approached Melisande and attempted to remove her belt.

"Nay!" she shouted and placed her hands over her middle, backing away from him.

Corin caught up with her and pried her arms away without any effort whatsoever. He tore the belt from her, bruising the sides of her ribs, then proceeded to rip her tunic down the front as if it were a sheet of parchment. She tried with all her might to push him away, but he was by far stronger than she. He plucked her torn tunic from her body and kicked it along with the belt toward the door, leaving her with only her short chemise. Corin then ordered her to remove her leg coverings and boots. Melisande shook her head. Undaunted, he replied, "If you do not, I will. And what a pleasure it will be." He eyed her up and down as he was wont to do of late, a leering grin touching the corners of his mouth.

Melisande leaned against the wall, groping at her hose and boots, tossing them at his feet.

"You are quite a vision, standing there in your undergarments that are so wet one could almost see right through them."

With a loud sob, Melisande covered her front with her arms.

Corin started toward her. She tried to step away but his hands landed on either side of her on the wall behind.

"Tonight you will be so cold, you will come to my bed willingly," he said in a low voice.

"Never!" she shouted. "I should like to freeze to death before—" Her loud declaration was interrupted when the unmistakable clatter of steel came from the corridor.

Corin cocked his head and considered the sound for a moment, then turned back to Melisande. "Do not try to run away again. I am posting two guards on the path below. I will most likely not see you again until you crawl under my coverlet this night." He pushed away from the wall and, with a slight bow in her direction, bade her farewell. Corin kicked the furs and the wet garments out of the door and shut it. She listened as the timber plank slammed into place and shivered.

Just then, Jeremy pushed his way through the small window above and Melisande stepped into the center of the room, looking up at him as he stood on the ledge. She stared at him, noting the strong similarities between the twins—their manners of speech as well as their features—save for the scruffy visage of Jeremy.

"It seems someone else wants Dupree for themselves, but I am confident that my men can take care of things." Jeremy jumped down, tossed his sword to the floor and started toward her. "I thought that while they are winning the battle downstairs, I shall claim you as a prize for myself." Taking a slow, lingering visual assessment, he added crudely, "I see that someone has made you ready for me. I should find them later and offer my thanks."

Melisande glanced at her surroundings and realized that there was nowhere for her to run. In seconds his arms had encircled her, his body pressing against hers. A scream welled up in her lungs and she let it loose like a flaming arrow. Jeremy tried to cover her scream with his mouth but Melisande bit his lip. His blood oozed between their faces. He pulled away, grunted, touched his lip and smiled at her. He then grabbed her hands, which clung to her chemise, and forced her to the cold stone floor. He moved on top of her and uttered against her ear, "The very sound of battle makes me hard."

"Nay!" Melisande screamed. At the same time, she heard someone shout her name.

Jeremy started to raise the hem of her chemise when a noise at the window stopped him. They both glanced up to find Sir Devin Blackburn dropping to the floor, his sword in hand. He looked to Melisande like a dark avenging angel.

"Blackburn," Jeremy said, smiling, rolling from their horizontal position. He jumped up and retrieved his sword from the floor.

"Sinclair, ready yourself for a second defeat," Devin murmured confidently.

Melisande scrambled to her feet and pressed her back to the door. At the first clash of weapons, Melisande covered her ears with both hands. The two large men were matched evenly and for every blow that was given, one was returned with the same force. They circled each other, waiting for an opportunity to attack. Jeremy lunged at Devin and they fell to the floor with a great thud. Their swords fell away and they each grabbed a handful of the other's clothing. As the two men exchanged fisted blows, they scraped across the floor, but could go no farther than the stone wall would allow.

Jeremy retrieved a concealed dagger from his boot and stabbed Devin in the arm through his chain mail.

Devin gritted his teeth and an anguished sound escaped his throat. He shoved the small weapon away. Blood gushed from his wound and he sneered at Jeremy.

In one swift movement, Devin lunged at Jeremy. Raging fury shone on Devin's face as he took hold of the man who'd attempted to ravish her. He lifted the villain up and slammed him head first into the wall.

Life and strength seemed to leave Jeremy as he lay upon the floor.

Devin rolled away from him and came to his feet. He turned to Melisande and started toward her.

Still frozen in horror, she managed to point at Jeremy. Devin got to his feet and turned to find Jeremy, whose blood ran profusely from a wound somewhere on the top of his head. He threw his dagger at Devin's back. However, it being a weak toss, the dagger fell to the floor, missing its mark. Devin picked the blade up and flung it back at Jeremy, who took it in the heart.

Melisande stood by the door shivering, unaware until now that she had been sobbing aloud while the men fought.

As if the clouds had moved away from the sun on purpose, light filled the dreary room through the high window and with it lifted an imaginary shroud from her eyes. Knight or not, she could not bear to exist without the man before her. She had been horribly deceived by beauty and courtly manners and needed to confess all to him. Somehow, through the madness that not moments ago had threatened to overtake her mind, she tried to find her voice, but it was too much too soon. A tunnel of black swallowed up her vision, and she was unable to stop it. Somewhere in the back of her mind she felt Devin take her up in his arms.

"Hush now, love. Dupree is safe," he cooed to her.

Melisande wept, but did not speak for quite some time.

Devin held her close and whispered tenderly, "I vow here and now with my body, heart and soul to protect you. Always. You've had my heart since I first heard your voice at the Willowbrook games," he said, his lips brushing lightly against her temple. "When I heard you call out to me over the wall at Windsor, it took all that I had within me not to turn back and run to you." His voice turned tremulous. "My lady, my love, you are my life. I'd be the worst of fools not to take you to wife."

From the outside, the bar was lifted noisily from the door. Parker entered with much haste and observed the body of Jeremy Sinclair, lifeless against the wall. "From the look of this room, I can attest to the fact that both of the Sinclairs are dead and their York cohorts are either dead as well or running in different directions through the countryside. We have dispatched messengers to the King at Windsor with the report." He stood there with his hands on his hips. "Dupree will be set to rights once again, m'lady, be assured of that. Even as we speak, thine household is returning from the stables where they were being held." He then returned his attention to Devin. "The war between the King's knights and the Yorkist traitors has been a sweet victory, wouldst thou not agree, Sir Devin?"

"Devin, that was beautiful." She realized too late that the moment she and Devin had just shared was now shattered to pieces, but she couldn't bear to let it go so easily.

Devin cleared his throat. With a sheepish grin, he looked at Parker and shrugged.

"Methinks her head is overly chilled," Parker said, obviously referring to her comment and state of undress.

Devin tossed his head toward the door. But just before Parker took his leave, he kicked the earlier discarded furs from outside the door toward them.

Wrapped in the furs and in Devin's arms, Melisande felt the warmth of his love welling up in her heart. They stayed thus for a short while until she spoke again. "Devin?"

"Aye, my lady love?" he answered, his head pressed to hers.

"I must tell you something."

"I am listening."

"I'm afraid you will not like what I have to say."

"Go on," he urged.

Melisande took a breath, but she knew that there was no delaying the inevitable. She forged ahead. "I almost married Corin Sinclair." She braced herself for his wrath, but when it did not come, she pulled her head away from his to look upon his face and assess his feelings.

"It would not have happened," he replied, dismissing the subject with a wave of his hand.

"What? How—"

"I would never have allowed it to."

Melisande searched his eyes, looking for the truth, and hers filled once again with tears, for his integrity shone like fire.

"What, no contradictory words? No cheeky comebacks?"

Melisande considered that she was rather shrewish sometimes. "I do that often, do I not?"

He smiled. "Aye. However, 'tis most charming."

From the moment they'd met, he'd been able to steal the breath from her with just one look. Not knowing exactly how to voice her sentiment, she fumbled with words, which rarely happened. "I wish—I want you to know that everything I am—everything I have, is yours. My heart, my home—"

"Your heart I'll gladly accept, but your home is your own."

Does he not want Dupree? Is it not as grand as Willowbrook? "Would I be imposing upon you were you to be my lord, then?"

He chuckled, leaned toward her and gave her a nudge with his forehead. "Do you have any idea how much I love you?"

Melisande's heart melted at his tender words, and at the same time her entire body surged to life. She reached up, entwining her arms around his neck.

"May I show you how much?"

Melisande nodded vigorously.

Devin carried her down the narrow stairway and she directed him to her room. He laid her upon the bed then kicked the door shut.

"Wait, let me fetch bindings for your arm," she offered, starting to rise from the bed.

"Nay, 'tis but a scratch." He deftly unstrapped and tossed aside his metal greaves then pulled off his boots. He presented his back to her. "Would you mind helping me out of this thing?" he asked regarding his chain mail.

After unlacing his coif, Melisande laboriously tried to remove the blackened metal shirt. "I cannot seem to lift... This...is heavy..."

Devin chuckled as he assisted her by bending at his waist. She tried to be mindful of his injury, but Devin merely shrugged out of the intricately linked metal rings as the mail shirt dropped to the floor.

"Am I to be your new squire then?" She grinned mischievously.

"Nay, never that, love. But you may undress me when we retire after we are married this very night," Devin said, shedding the rest of his overclothes. "If it is your wish as well, of course. And damn the banns," he added. "We've been through too much of late to wait. I'll bribe the friar with three barrels of mead — that should appease him."

She giggled her agreement then sobered. "I have always been yours, you know."

A low, sensual growl came from Devin's throat as he looked at Melisande from beneath hooded eyelids. "Come hither, wench."

Melisande dove under the coverlet, trying to dodge his already approaching hands. She did so love it when Devin chased her. She knew her reward would come when he caught her — and she planned on being caught each and every time he gave chase for the rest of her life.

"Ho there, woman. Where do you think you are going?" He caught her by the ankle and she squealed with delight. He positioned her on the mattress next to where he stood.

"Your wound! You'll bleed to death." She tried to sound serious, but she was too delighted to do so.

He plucked at the ties of his trews and in seconds his hose slid down his legs. He kicked them away and discarded the rest of his garments. "I appreciate your concern, but more than worry about my death, I need to be inside you. This very moment. Or my death will have nothing to do with loss of blood."

She wiggled out of her chemise. While she did so, she took in the vision before her. God's teeth, but he was splendid. His thick cock stood at the ready and a hot wetness seeped from between her thighs at the sight of it.

At once he turned her so that her feet dangled off the side of the bed. His hands slid beneath her knees and he tugged. She thought she might fall from the bed as her bottom hung precariously close to the edge. She closed her eyes and waited for his invasion.

"My love?" His voice sounded with such tenderness that it made her breath catch. She peered up at him.

"Aye?"

"They didn't...hurt you, did they?"

"Nay." She shook her head. "I am unspoilt."

"That is not what I meant." He reached down and caressed her cheek. "No matter what, I will always want you." Then he added, "I only wanted to know because... Well, I'm not sure how gentle I should be right now."

She couldn't keep from smiling. "Don't you dare be gentle."

He returned her grin. "You wicked girl."

"If you don't hurry, I'll turn into a wicked old crone right before your eyes."

A sound tore from his throat that sounded like pained laughter and he drove his cock into her.

Melisande's body reacted, her hips cradling his with each blow and grind her lover delivered. Pleasure radiated from where they were joined, sending lightning bolts to her every limb as she clung to him. He'd saved her from a fate she wouldn't have been able to escape from on her own and now here he was, delivering her body from loneliness and despair in such a hedonistic way she thought she'd die any moment. If hell awaited her, she vowed, lost in his intimate embrace would indeed be worth the eternal exchange.

She reached up and drove her fingers into the hair at the nape of his neck, scratching his scalp with her nails.

He paused and looked down at her, inhaling a long, hissing breath through his teeth. "My sweet wench." He grinned. "Getting rough, are we?"

"I thought you might need some encouragement in that department."

"Encouragement?"

"Or, mayhaps, assistance?"

He ground into her then. "Oh, my lady, I assure you, I need no assistance whatsoever."

Devin increased his cadence and Melisande felt reality slip away. Each stroke hurled her higher and higher, her voice resonating with ecstasy.

In her euphoria she cried out. "Aye, Devin."

"You are mine." He pumped hard into her. "Ever mine, love."

The crescendo shattered her, her insides milking his cock, drawing on his seed.

"Melisande—" He groaned and his body trembled against hers as he climaxed.

After a few moments passed, he settled with her in the center of the bed and pulled the coverlet over them both. He pulled her close and sighed. And a joyful sound it was. She couldn't have agreed more.

Just then, Maggie and Tilly burst into the room.

"Oh, my lady! We were sore afraid you'd—" Tilly's words stalled in her throat.

Maggie's eyes widened. "But that's not the one—" Tilly's elbow connected with Maggie's side, abruptly stopping her verbal observation.

"Nay, Maggie," Melisande murmured, "but it is the *right* one."

Devin cleared his throat and the girls, after one more glance at him, lowered their gazes. "Send for the friar at once."

"Aye, my lord." They both curtsied and rushed from the room, closing the door behind them.

Grinning, Melisande rolled onto her side and Devin followed, snuggling against her backside.

"I love you," he whispered.

"I love you, too."

With her body sated, and her soon-to-be husband — of her own choosing — clasped to her as if he'd never let go, she felt, for the very first time in her life, genuinely overwhelmed with joy.

Utterly. Blissfully. Happy.

Glossary of Medieval Terms

Grammercy—short for God grant thee mercy, also means thank you

Lists—an enclosed arena for jousting, also can mean the barriers enclosing said arena

Malmsey—a strong, sweet wine

Psaltery—a medieval musical instrument played by plucking the strings

Sennight—seven nights (one week)

Verily—in truth or certainly

About the Author

Born and reared in Southern California, Genella DeGrey longed to be your typical blonde, tanned, surfer girl but failed miserably. Unable to sit idle without falling asleep, she embarked upon several artistic endeavors. Make-up and set dressing for the entertainment industry, Resort Enhancement for The Walt Disney Company and writing sexy historical romance top the list of her favorite activities. A consummate closet goth and amateur music and (red) wine enthusiast, she is also a hopeless romantic awaiting the arrival of her very own Mr Romance/Soul Mate with whom to share the rest of her life.

Genella DeGrey loves to hear from readers. You can find her contact information, website and author biography at http://www.totallybound.com